Julian Hawthorne

Yellow-cap and other fairy-stories for children

Julian Hawthorne

Yellow-cap and other fairy-stories for children

ISBN/EAN: 9783744749213

Printed in Europe, USA, Canada, Australia, Japan

Cover: Foto ©Andreas Hilbeck / pixelio.de

More available books at **www.hansebooks.com**

YELLOW-CAP

&c.

LONDON: PRINTED BY
SPOTTISWOODE AND CO., NEW-STREET SQUARE
AND PARLIAMENT STREET

YELLOW-CAP

AND OTHER FAIRY-STORIES FOR CHILDREN

BY

JULIAN HAWTHORNE

LONDON

LONGMANS, GREEN, AND CO.

1880

CONTENTS.

YELLOW-CAP.

RUMPTY-DUDGET.

CALLADON.

THEEDA.

YELLOW-CAP.

CHAPTER I.

A GOOD many years ago—before Julius Cæsar landed at Dover, in fact, and while the architect's plans for Stonehenge were still under consideration—England was inhabited by a civilised and prosperous people, who did not care about travelling, and who were renowned for their affability to strangers. The climate was warm and equable; there were no fogs, no smoke, no railways, and no politics. The Government was an absolute monarchy; one king, who was by birth and descent an Englishman, lived in London all the year round; and as for London, it was the cleanest, airiest, and most beautiful city in the whole world.

A few miles outside of the city walls lay a small village called Honeymead. It had some fifteen or twenty thatched cottages, each with its vegetable garden and its bee-

hives, its hencoop and its cowshed.   Around
this village fertile meadows spread down to
the river banks, bringing forth plenteous crops
for the support of the honest and thrifty hus-
bandmen who tilled them.   There was only
one public-house in the place, and the only
drink to be had there was milk.   A case of
drunkenness was, consequently, seldom heard
of; though, on the other hand, women, girls,
and even small children might be seen lin-
gering about the place as well as men.

   This public-house was called the Brindled Cow, and it was kept by a young
woman whose name was Rosamund.   She
was the prettiest maiden in the village, as
well as the most good-natured and the
thriftiest ; though she had a keen tongue of
her own' when occasion demanded. As might
be supposed, all the young men in the neigh-
bourhood were anxious to marry her ; but
she gave them little or no encouragement.
She used to tell them that she was well able
to take care of herself, so what good would a
husband be to her ?   She didn't want to support him, and she didn't need his support. It
was better as it was.   As for falling in love,
that was a thing she couldn't pretend to under-

stand ; but her maiden aunt had once told her
that it was more bother than it was worth,
and she thought it very likely. Moreover, if
by any accident she should one day happen
to fall in love, she would take great care that
it should not be suspected, because the man
she loved would then become so puffed up
with conceit there'd be no bearing him !

Such was Rosamund's declared opinion
upon matrimony ; and it caused gloom to
dwell in the heart of many a love-sick swain.
But (what was strange) the more love-sick
they grew the fatter and rosier they became.
The reason probably was that they were for
ever going to the Brindled Cow under pre-
tence of being thirsty—but in reality to feast
their eyes on Rosamund's lovely face ; and
since, thirsty or not, she insisted upon their
drinking, as long as they stayed, at the rate
of a pint of rich unskimmed milk every ten
minutes, you will easily understand that it
soon became possible to measure the ardour
of their affection in pounds avoirdupois. So
that by-and-by, when the elders of the village would see their sons waxing great of
girth and blowzy of visage, they would shake
their heads and murmur sadly—

'Ah! poor lad, how healthy he's getting! 'Tis plain he's in love with Mistress Rosamund!'

There was one young fellow, however, who was seldom seen among the tipplers at the Brindled Cow. He was a slender youth, rather pale, with straight black eyebrows and large thoughtful eyes, which always seemed to be gazing at something far away. There was a romantic story about him, which you shall hear. When he was a small child, only three years old, his mother (who took in washing, and would be called a laundress nowadays) was up to her elbows one Tuesday afternoon in soapsuds and shirts; and Raymond—that was the child's name—was sitting beside the washing-tub, blowing soap-bubbles. All of a sudden the tramp of a horse was heard in the street without, and the woman, looking up from her scrubbing-board, had a glimpse through the window of a magnificent horseman, in silk and velvet, with rosettes on his shoulders, and wearing a gold cap with a tall peacock's feather in it. He got off his horse; and in another moment he had opened the cottage door and walked into the washing-room.

The poor woman was at first vastly frightened, for she thought this must be the King, and that he was going to cut off her head because she used chemicals in her washing—though she had never done such a thing except when she was very much pressed for time, or when the water was so hard that the soap would not make suds. However, like a wise woman as she was, she made up her mind not to ask for mercy until she had heard her accusation; so she dropped half a dozen curtseys, and begged to know what his Gracious Royal Majesty's Highness wanted.

Meanwhile, the little boy, from his seat beside the wash-tub, stared and stared at the magnificent stranger, and was sure he never could stare at him enough. The stranger was tall, thin, and as straight as a hop-pole; had a huge aquiline nose, with a pair of long moustachios jutting out beneath it and curling up to his eyes; and on his chin was a sharp-pointed beard. The steam from the wash-tub filled the little room and swam in misty clouds round this singular figure; while the last soap-bubble which the little boy had blown from his pipe rose in the air and

circled round and round the yellow cap like a
planet round the sun. Altogether he looked
like an Eastern genie in an English court-
dress—an uncommon sight in the times I
write of.

This personage now made two profound
obeisances, one to the washerwoman and one
to the little boy. This done, he threw back
his silk-lined cloak, and taking from the
pocket of his doublet a bundle of something
done up in gold paper, he opened his mouth
and said—

'O yez! O yez! O yez! Whereas his
Transparent Majesty King Ormund, Emperor of Great Britain, France, and Ireland,
Defender of the Faith, and so forth, and so
forth, did, while riding through this village
called Honeymead, splash with mud his left
Transparent stocking : now, therefore, O
washerwoman, it is his gracious will and pleasure that you do hereby wash the same, with
all due and proper diligence and despatch, and
with the smallest possible amount of unne-
cessary procrastination. Long live his Trans-
parency King Ormund !'

In fact, the gold paper contained a fine
pink silk stocking, with embroidered clocks,

a hole in the toe, and seven spots of mud spattered over it. The washerwoman had understood very little of the speech, but she could see that the stocking needed washing; so without more ado she plunged it into the soapsuds, and in five minutes it was as clean as the day it came out of the shop, and was dried before the fire. All this time the stranger had stood bolt upright in the centre of the little room, swathed in the steam, and with the soap-bubble still revolving round his head like a planet; and the little boy still stared up at him, as if he never could stare enough.

When the stocking was quite dry the washerwoman rolled it up again in the gold paper and gave it to the stranger, who put it back in the pocket of his doublet. Then he took from the purse that hung at his belt a new spade guinea, gave it a fillip into the air, and down it fell in the little boy's lap. Then, with a third profound obeisance, he made a long step back towards the door.

Up jumped the little boy in a great hurry and excitement.

'If you please, sir,' he cried out, 'who are you?'

The stranger stopped ; and as the steam from the wash-tub wound around him more and more, and the soap-bubble burst on the bridge of his aquiline nose, he replied—

'Little boy, I am an Appanage of Royalty!'

'Please will you give me your yellow cap?' asked Raymond again.

'Not to-day,' said the Appanage of Royalty, with a queer smile.

'To-morrow, then?' demanded Raymond.

'Some day—perhaps!' the other replied, still with that queer smile. And then he disappeared ; but whether he dissolved into steam, or exploded like a soap-bubble, or went out by the door in the regular way, the little boy could never be quite sure. It was enough for him that an Appanage of Royalty had said that some day, perhaps, he would give him his gold cap. And Raymond never forgot this adventure ; and as a kind of pledge of its reality he ever afterwards wore the spade guinea round his neck by a silken string. He believed that sooner or later it would be the means of bringing him fame and greatness.

CHAPTER II.

ONE fine May morning, while Rosamund was churning in the dairy-room of the Brindled Cow, she heard some one walk into the bar. The step was not that of any one of her familiar suitors. It was neither short plump Armand, nor tall bulky Osmund, nor red-haired broad-cheeked Phillimund, nor short-legged thick-necked Sigismund, who drank six quarts of milk last Saturday; nor short-breathed apoplectic Dorimund, who sang sentimental songs with a voice like a year-old heifer's. No, none of these had a step like this step—sauntering, light, and meditative. Nevertheless, it was a step which Rosamund loved to hear.

She stopped churning, and moved softly to where a brightly-polished tin pan was set up on the shelf. It was Rosamund's looking-

glass. Before this she smoothed her rumpled
hair, straightened the pink bow at her throat,
and snatched off her dirty apron. She was
provoked to see how red the churning had
made her cheeks, and she wished she were
paler ; but the wish only seemed to make
her rosier than before. She told herself that
she was a coarse-looking ugly girl ; and yet
when, only that morning, Dorimund had told
her that she was as beautiful as a fairy, she
had taken it quite as a matter of course. It
was tiresome—the way people could grow
ugly all in a moment—and in the wrong moment too !

All this happened during the two or three
minutes after the light-stepping visitor had
come into the bar; and now this person
tapped twice or thrice on the counter. Rosamund, on hearing the tap, began to hum a
little song, in an unconcerned sort of way,
and walked up and down the dairy a few
times, as if she were putting things in order;
and when, at last, she came out to the bar,
it was with the air of a very busy young
woman, who does not like to be disturbed at
her churning.

'Oh, is it you ? ' she said to the person

who was leaning on the counter. 'How do you do? I hope you're thirsty?'

The person smiled. He was a handsome young fellow, with dark hair and a pale face, and he looked at Rosamund with a pair of thoughtful eyes. His dress was plain and rather the worse for wear; but round his neck a bright spade guinea was hung by a silken string. It did not seem different from any other spade guinea, yet there must have been something peculiar about it. For it gave a kind of dignity to the young man's aspect, so that if you fixed your eyes upon the coin you forgot the wearer's shabbiness, and almost fancied him to be a noble and opulent personage. Whether the owner were aware of this or not is another question; but, as a general thing, young people seldom know what it is about them that makes them attractive.

'I hope you are thirsty?' Rosamund repeated, in a business-like tone, as she leaned against the other side of the counter, and looked up at the young man with her lovely blue eyes.

'I am not thirsty, Rosamund,' he replied, 'but I am tired.'

'I've always heard that doing nothing was tiresome. Perhaps you'd like to take a chair and sit down? I really must go on with my churning.'

'It isn't that kind of tired that I mean, said he; 'but if you'll let me sit down in the dairy I don't mind.' Rosamund made no objection, so he vaulted over the counter and they went into the dairy together. 'I'm so tired waiting!' he added, with a sigh.

'And what are you waiting for, may I ask?'

'For something great to happen!'

'Oh! Then why don't you make it happen?'

'I wish I could!' sighed the young man.

Rosamund tied her apron on again, and laid hold of the churn-handle.

'What do you call great?' she asked, beginning to work it up and down.

The young man took his gold coin meditatively between his thumb and forefinger and twisted it on its silken string.

'Greatness is everything that I have not, and want to have,' he said.

'Such as what?'

'Oh, power and wealth, and to be above other men, and to have them look up to me and obey me. That is greatness.'

'Pooh!' exclaimed Rosamund, working her churn vigorously. 'I shouldn't care about such greatness as that.'

'Not care about it, Rosamund?'

'Not so much as a pat of butter, Raymond. What do you want of wealth? Are you hungry, pray, or thirsty? I will give you as much of the best milk, fresh from the cow, as you can drink; and all the wealth in the world couldn't help you to drink more. As for power—however high it brought you, it couldn't make you yourself higher by so much as a single inch : you would still be the same Raymond you are now, even if you were an emperor—yes, or that Appanage of Royalty you've been thinking and talking about all these dozen years or more. Why do you want people to look up to you and obey you, I should like to know? Can't you see that it's not you they would look up to, but your ermine robe and silk stockings——'

'Ah! my mother once washed one of the King's silk stockings—the left one,' murmured Raymond ; 'and the Appanage of Royalty

said that some day, perhaps, he would give
me his yellow cap——'

'And golden crown,' continued Rosamund, not noticing the interruption. 'You
silly boy! they would obey the crown, not
you, though you might happen to be wearing
it. If you think it would be yourself they
cared for, just go to London as you are
now and order them about! But if I were
you I'd rather be truly loved by one—person than be obeyed by one hundred thousand.'

'But if you were I, Rosamund, you'd be
a man; and men are different.'

'So it seems.'

'What a noise that churn makes! Rosamund, I've felt all my life long that I was
destined to be great. Why else did my
mother wash the King's stocking; or the
Appanage of Royalty promise me the
cap?'

'You've been dreaming, you silly boy!'

'But can a dream that I've been dreaming
all my life fail to come true? I don't say
that to sit on a throne and rule a kingdom
would be the happiest lot in the world; but,
just as an experience, it would be good fun;

and if one is predestined to it, you know——
Besides——'

'Well, your majesty—besides what?'

'Well, for instance, how would you like to
be a queen?'

Rosamund stopped churning, wiped her
hands on her apron, and tossed up her pretty
chin with a saucy air.

'A queen, indeed! I beg to inform you,
Master Raymond, that I am a queen already,
and I have reigned longer and more despoti-
cally than ever you will, I fancy. Pray, has
the Queen of England any subjects more
devoted to her than my Osmund and Dorimund and Phillimund and Sigismund and
Armand, and twenty others, are to me?
Honeymead is my kingdom, and I do really
reign, because my power is in myself; and
fifty giants to march before me, and a
hundred dwarfs to carry my train, wouldn't
make me a bit more of a queen than I am
now. So—thank you for nothing, Master
Raymond!'

Raymond sat erect, with a great deal
more animation in his look than he had yet
shown.

'Listen to me, Rosamund,' he cried. 'It

C

is true you are Queen of Honeymead. But
what is Honeymead compared with London ?
And why should not you be as much a queen
in London as you are here ?   You would be
none the worse for a crown, and dwarfs and
giants, though you might not need them : because no man could look at you and not be
your faithful subject ever afterwards.   And
—Rosamund——'

He hesitated, and his cheeks were quite
red.   Rosamund glanced up at him and
thought, ' How handsome he is ! '

' Rosamund, I ask you this : if I become
king will you sit beside me on the throne,
and rule over Great Britain, France, and
Ireland ? '

Rosamund looked very grave.

' Do you mean to ask me to be your wife,
Raymond ? ' she asked.

' I would have asked you long before,
dearest Rosamund, but I waited hoping to be
able to offer you a kingdom along with my
love.'

' Well, it is a very kind offer,' said she,
with a little smile and a sigh, ' and I thank
you.   But I must say no.'

' Rosamund ! '

'If I were your wife I should have no time to attend to the duties of the Court; and if I were your queen I should have no time to attend to you. And I am so jealous that I could not let you neglect me for your kingdom; and yet I'm so ambitious that I couldn't let you neglect your kingdom for me. So it would not do either way; and, if you please, we won't talk any more about it.'

But as she said this her voice trembled, and tears were in her eyes. Then Raymond's heart overflowed with tenderness, and he went to her and took her hand.

'I could not be happy on a throne with-out you, Rosamund,' said he; 'but I could be happy, if you would marry me, without a throne.'

And because it cost him a good deal to make this sacrifice (even of something he had not got) his voice trembled a little too.

When Rosamund heard that she could resist no longer. She smiled such a smile as Dorimund and the rest would have given their farms to win from her; and said she—

'Oh, Raymond! I am a greater queen in having your love than——'

And then Raymond kissed her just on

the place that the next word was coming out of, so the rest of the sentence was lost.

'But are you quite sure, dear Raymond, that you will be content to live here always?' she asked, when they had had a little more conversation of this kind.

Raymond smiled down on her, but he said nothing. Perhaps, in his secret heart, he was thinking that Destiny (which had appeared to him in the shape of the Appanage of Royalty so long ago) might still have some splendid gift in store for him and Rosamund, whereof the yellow cap would be but the symbol. And, if so, it would be foolish in them to bind themselves beforehand not to take advantage of it. So Raymond smiled at Rosamund in a way to show that, at all events, he loved her. And he did love her, no doubt.

'Poor boy!' said Rosamund, after another pause, smiling back rather mischievously, 'to think that you have been wearing this spade guinea all these years, and it has brought you nothing better than me at last!'

'If guineas could buy girls like you, my dear,' replied Raymond, 'the Mint would be kept working day and night. But I'll tell you what use we will make of this—we'll chop it in two, and each of us will wear a half, in token that we belong to one another. And then, no matter how long we may be separated, or what changes come over us, we should always recognise each other by these bits of gold.'

'But you don't think that changes will come over us, or that we shall be separated, Raymond?'

'Certainly not; but we may as well be on the safe side. For instance, if I were to go out and meet with an enchanter, and he were to turn me into a dwarf, and then I were to come back to you, how would you know me except by my half of the guinea?'

'I should trust my heart for that,' said Rosamund, softly. 'Still, we will wear the halves, so that everyone may see that we are but half ourselves when we are not together.'

This being settled, Rosamund fetched a hatchet, and Raymond put the guinea on a stool, and, with one strong blow, made it fly into two exact halves. Then he drilled a hole through Rosamund's half, and hung it round her neck by a piece of pink ribbon; and as for his own half, he strung it on the silken cord that he had always worn. So their betrothal was confirmed.

Just at this moment half a dozen of Rosamund's old suitors came trooping into the bar, and began calling for milk like a herd of calves. Then the lovers looked in each other's faces and smiled, and bade each other farewell very tenderly. Raymond went out through the cowyard ; and Rosamund returned to the bar, where she served out fresh milk and thought about the half-guinea that was hidden in her bosom.

CHAPTER III.

THE GOLDEN DWARF.

RAYMOND strolled away towards the river.
He wanted to think it all over. His betrothal was a sort of surprise to him. He had
loved Rosamund, in a meditative way, so
long that he had got used to not expecting
anything more ; but now, on the spur of the
moment, he had told his love and received
the pledge of hers, and it was all settled. He
was happy, of course, for he believed Rosamund to be the prettiest and the best girl in
the world. Still, he did not wish quite to
give up the hope that something might happen to make their life more splendid. He
said to himself that it was only for Rosamund's sake he hoped this. Perhaps that
was the reason he hoped it so much.

The path down to the river was narrow
and winding ; it lay between hawthorn hedges

white with blossoms. It ended at the ford, where willow trees bowed down over the current. One of these trees had been cut down on the day Raymond was born. The stump made a sort of chair, in which Raymond had spent many a summer hour, musing over the flowing water, or lifting his eyes to gaze thoughtfully at the distant city. He called the willow-stump his throne; and in the stream that hurried beneath he imagined he saw the march of mighty nations passing before his feet to do him homage. To-day all such imaginations must end; and it was more habit than anything else that had brought him to the spot. He did not come, as formerly, half in fear and half in delight, hoping to meet with some beneficent fairy or other, who would grant him the three wishes which all fairies have in their gift. No; he came to take a last look at that world of dreams in which he had lived from childhood, and to make up his mind to living henceforth in the matter-of-fact world which common people inhabited.

It was afternoon when he came to the willow-stump throne and sat down upon it. The sky was thronged with stately clouds—

phantom mountains, with castles on their tops—castles wherein Raymond's fancy had often dwelt. The air was soft and warm, sweet with fragrance of lilac and apple-blossoms, and bright with bird-songs. The bending willows swept the river surface with slender green fingers, startling the trout and grayling that quivered and darted in the pools and shallows. Life and beauty and happiness were everywhere ; and far to the eastward, piled high against the horizon, rose the white marble walls and towers of mighty London. They looked less real than the clouds. Sunlight sparkled on the gilded domes, and cast afar the tender purple shadows of royal palaces. And amidst green meadow-banks, and past gleaming wharves populous with delicate masts and rainbow sails, swept the azure curves of the translucent Thames towards the fair city. London was, indeed, at this time, the most magnificent city in the world ; and Camelot, which was built hundreds of years afterwards, was never anything to compare with it. What wonder, then, if Raymond eyed its distant splendours with some regret, remembering that they were lost to him for ever ?

'But I have Rosamund,' he murmured to himself.

'So much the more fool you!' spoke a metallic voice close behind him.

Raymond looked round. Whence had come that grotesque figure which was standing within a couple of yards of him, and which gazed at him with an expression at once so quizzical and so penetrating? Had he ever seen it before? No—and yet—had he?

The figure was that of a man about three feet high, with a body shaped like a sack of potatoes, supported by short and crooked legs that bent beneath its weight. The arms were so long that the hands (like great curved claws) hung down nearly to the ground; and the fingers made a continual movement as if clutching something. The head of this creature was large, and had no neck; the nose was aquiline, the eyes bright and sharp. On the chin was a pointed beard, and a pair of long moustachios curled up over the cheek-bones. The creature was dressed in rich and costly clothes, which, however, bore an unaccountable resemblance to Raymond's own threadbare attire. On the head was a yellow cap, apparently made of woven gold, which glowed and sparkled in the sunlight. Certainly there was something familiar about that cap and those moustachios !

'Where did you come from ?' Raymond asked.

' I was here before you,' replied the dwarf.

' I saw no one.'

'People do overlook me sometimes,' rejoined the other, with a chuckle ; 'but they are more apt to spend their lives in trying to find me. Once in a great while I appear without being asked—as I do now !'

' Where have I seen you before ?'

' Ask yourself. '

'Who are you ?'

The dwarf made a low bow. 'I am an Appanage of Royalty !' said he.

'Then it was you who brought the King's silk stocking to be washed ! But were you not a great deal taller then than now ?'

'What of that ? Were not you a great deal shorter ?'

'That is true,' murmured Raymond, struck by the justness of the remark.

'True as gold !' added the dwarf, with

another chuckle. 'And so you want to go
to London?' he continued suddenly.

Raymond started. 'I have been thinking
of it,' he said; 'but now——'

'Nonsense! You want to go now as
much as before you went to the Brindled
Cow, and I am the only person in the world
that can help you do it.'

'But how did you know——'

'Pooh! I know everything. Weren't you
thinking of me at the very moment you kissed
her? There—no more words! Are you
ready to start? Speak up.'

But Raymond drew back, startled and
mystified. Seeing this, the dwarf altered his
tone, and from being abrupt and overbearing
became friendly and familiar.

'Come, my dear boy,' he said, laying his
great claw on Raymond's arm. 'Men must
be men; we mustn't let ourselves be ordered
about by a parcel of women. Would you let
a few kisses and keepsakes stand in the way
of your ambition? How many years has she
waited for you? Let her wait twenty-four
hours longer. Besides, if you don't go now
you will never go at all. Rosamond—trust
me—will like you none the less when she

sees you the greatest man in England. Come, now. I can put in your hands a power before which the whole world bows : will you take it or not ? I shan't offer it twice.'

Now, Raymond had a secret suspicion that something was wrong in all this ; for why should a stranger be so anxious to confer an inestimable boon upon him ? And yet London was but seven miles off. He could get back that very night if need be. It would be a pity to lose this chance after having waited for it so long. It could do no harm ; it was worth trying. ' I think I will,' passed through Raymond's mind.

' I knew you would!' exclaimed the dwarf at once, as if Raymond had spoken aloud. ' But we must lose no time, for you must be in London by five ; that is the hour when the Seven Brethren assemble. So—off with your doublet !'

' Why must I take my doublet off ? '

' To exchange with me. Mine is the same as yours—the only difference is in the lining. Try it.'

' But it's too small,' objected Raymond.

' It will fit whomsoever is lucky enough

to get it,' said the dwarf, wagging his big head confidently. 'Let me help you—first this arm—then this—and there you are.' And there Raymond was, sure enough, as neatly fitted as if he had been to the Court tailor.

'And now, my dear Raymond,' continued the dwarf affably, 'I must trouble you to carry me across the ford. One—two—and there we are!' And before the astonished young man had time to remonstrate his new friend had sprang upon his shoulders, wound his long arms about his neck, and was urging him into the water.

Well, it would not be so much of a job to carry over so small a creature, Raymond thought. Besides, since putting on the dwarf's doublet he had felt less his own master than before. If his soul were still his own his doublet was not; and a very small compromise of freedom sometimes goes a long way. So Raymond (like his contemporary Sindbad the Sailor) set forth meekly with his burden on his back.

The River Thames was, in those days, very clear and transparent, with a sandy bottom, and with frequent shallows or fords. The Honeymead ford was reckoned an especially good one ; and Raymond, expecting an easy passage, stepped into the eddying current with confidence.

But before he had gone far he thought there must be a mistake somewhere : either he was not so strong as he had supposed or else the dwarf was uncommonly heavy. Twice or thrice he staggered and almost lost his footing. By the time he had got to the middle of the stream every muscle in his body ached, his legs trembled under him, and the sweat stood on his forehead. The water, too, rose high above his waist, and seemed to flow with unusual swiftness. If he had been carrying a sack of gold on his shoulders, instead of a dwarf, it could not have felt heavier.

' You're not tired ? ' asked the dwarf, as Raymond laid hold of a rock that rose partly out of the water and panted as if his lungs would burst.

'What on earth are you made of ?' gasped the young man.

' Of all things conducive to worldly prosperity,' said the other, with his odd metallic chuckle. ' But now, as we are at the middle of the river, let us settle the terms of our bargain. I will give you my cap—you have wanted it ever since that day in the washing-room—in exchange for yours.' Having made this exchange (which Raymond was, of course, powerless to prevent his doing, even had he been so inclined), the dwarf continued : ' You now possess the most precious talisman in the world. By making a proper use of that cap you may reach any height of fortune. Does it fit you comfortably ? '

' Not at all ! ' cried Raymond : ' it makes my head ache. Take it off again.'

' Pooh ! my good Raymond, is not un-bounded wealth worth a headache ? Besides, you will get used to it after a while. Mean-time listen to this couplet, which contains much wisdom in small space :—

> Cap on—cap and knee !
> Cap off—who is he?

Can you remember that ? '

' What if I can ? ' groaned Raymond, clinging to the rock. ' We shall both be drowned in another minute ! '

' Not at all,' answered the dwarf with composure. ' My left foot is a trifle wet ; but what of that ? By-the-by, I shall be passing through Honeymead again this evening; shall I drop in at the Brindled Cow and tell Rosamund that you are all right?'

'I am not all right. I wish I were at the Brindled Cow myself.'

'Tut! tut! Ambition should not be so easily damped. Well, I'll make a point of calling on the young lady. But, stay; I must carry some token to prove that I am an authorised messenger. What shall it be? Ah! this will do—this half of a spade guinea that you wear at your neck. Permit me to remove it.' And he began to fumble with the silken string.

'Stop! that is my betrothal pledge—you can't have that!' cried Raymond, putting up his hand to withhold the dwarf's claw.

'And who was it gave it to you, in the first place, I should like to know?' exclaimed the dwarf tartly. 'Fie! have you so little confidence in your friends? It is for your own good that I must have the token. Give it me at once.'

The place in which this discussion was carried on was so inconvenient to Raymond, he was getting so exhausted, both in body and mind, and the dwarf had spoken the last sentence so imperiously, that Raymond thought he had better yield. Moreover, the yellow cap squeezed his brain just in those places where the proper arguments lay, and thus prevented his using them. The end of it was that he said—

'I suppose you'd better take it, but——'

He never finished his sentence. The dwarf whipped the silken string over his head, and the golden pledge was gone. The next moment Raymond was floundering headlong in the stream. How he reached the opposite bank he never knew—he seemed to be under the water half the time. At last he got his hands on a bush growing beside the margin and pulled himself out.

Where was the dwarf? He had vanished. Had he fallen off and been drowned? What was that echo of a metallic chuckle in the air? Raymond groaned and pressed his hands to his aching head, on which the yellow cap stuck fast.

CHAPTER IV.

THE TALISMAN.

AFTER a while he got up and looked about him. The river was much swollen, and was hurrying past its banks with such fury that it was useless to think of returning as he had come. No, he must go on. His head was confused, so that he could not think clearly about Honeymead, and still less about Rosamund. She seemed far away and indistinct. Did she love him? Did he love her? At all events, it was better to fix his mind on London now. He looked thither, but the clouds had gathered over the sky, and the sunlight no longer gleamed upon the golden pinnacles. The city did not seem so alluring as from the other side of the river. However, time was flying, and London was seven miles away. Raymond set forth.

By and by he came to a milestone, on which he sat down to rest, and to wonder

D 2

how he was to make his fortune in London
when he got there. It was true that he had
a talisman, but how was that to help him?
A yellow cap! It was, indeed, woven of
golden thread, and might be sold for a
guinea; but a guinea was not a kingdom.
Meanwhile the cap made his head ache so
that he pulled it off. It was certainly a fine
cap. It was lined with the best yellow satin,
and a peacock's feather was stuck in the
band. On the band some letters were em-
.broidered. Raymond spelt them out, and
found that they made the following couplet :—

> Cap on—cap and knee !
> Cap off—who is he ?

It was the same that the dwarf had repeated to him in the river. What did it
mean? The dwarf had said it was full of
wisdom; but Raymond had never been much
in the way of wisdom, and perhaps might fail
to recognise it when he saw it. He could
not even be sure whether it were better
wisdom to put the cap on again or to keep
it off. He was inclined to keep it off. His
head felt much clearer so ; he was able to
think lovingly of Rosamund once more, and

he longed to see her again. What if some harm came to her in his absence? Might not that half of the spade guinea give the dwarf some power over her? He rose to his feet full of anxiety, and looked back towards Honeymead. Through a break in the clouds the sun lit up the little village; the cottages showed clearly in the warm light; and amongst them, with its thatched and gabled roof, and with the great lime-trees standing over it, was the Brindled Cow. Rosamund was there, no doubt, wondering where her Raymond was. Now, perhaps, the dwarf was coming in, with the half-guinea round his neck. What if he were to assert that he was the true Raymond, showing the token in proof thereof? When this thought came into Raymond's mind he started up from the milestone, resolved to go back to Honeymead without the loss of an instant. How blind and stupid he had been! Was not Rosamund more precious than a kingdom, or than all the money in the Bank of England? Of course she was!

But just as Raymond's eyes were sparkling with good resolutions, and one foot advanced on the way back to the Brindled

Cow, he heard a flourish of trumpets, haut-
boys, and cymbals, and, behold! a splendid
cavalcade advancing towards him on the way
to London. In front rode a company of
knights in glittering armour; then came a
long array of men-at-arms, squires, and attendants, gorgeously attired; then more
knights, riding two-and-two; then a body of
courtiers, and in the midst of these, borne
upon the shoulders of some of them, a platform draped in cloth of gold. Upon the
platform was a chair of carved ivory, and in
the chair sat a man with a long white beard
falling over his breast, and an ermine mantle
on his shoulders. One foot rested on a
golden footstool, thereby showing a fine silk
stocking with embroidered clocks. The sight
of that stocking made Raymond's heart beat.

By this time the vanguard of knights had
reached the milestone beside which Raymond
was standing. As they passed they glanced
at him contemptuously. This annoyed him,
for he was used to think well of himself, and
the Honeymead people treated him with
consideration. But if the knights looked
contemptuous, the men-at-arms and attendants jeered and made mouths at him; and

as for the pages they mocked and bantered him unmercifully.

'Here's an odd fish!' cried one, pointing with his finger.

'He's lost his way trying to swim on land!' laughed another.

'A scaly fellow—let's skin him and clean him!' called out a third.

'How much are you a pound, fish?' asked a fourth.

'Bah! he's stale already!' shouted a fifth.

'What's that in his right fin?—a human cap and feather, I declare!' exclaimed a sixth.

'Take it away from him!' cried several together; and one spurred his horse towards the young man and reached forth the point of his lance, as if to catch the cap from Raymond's hand.

But Raymond, though a minute ago he was almost ready to throw the cap away, was not going to submit to being robbed of it. He caught the lance by the shaft and jerked it from the page's grasp; then, putting the cap firmly on his head, he stood on his guard boldly, with the weapon advanced.

Why was the laugh with which the other pages had begun to greet their companion's mishap checked so suddenly ? Why was every eye bent upon Raymond with an expression of respect and subservience ? Why did all salute him so profoundly, bowing to their saddles in silent homage ? What did this sudden change mean ? It could not be that they were awed by the bold front he had shown ; it was more likely that this was but a new way of making fun of him. And yet it was odd that all should have joined in it unanimously and at an instant's notice. What did it all mean ?

The pages passed on, and the second company of knights followed. Strange ! they also seemed to have taken up the jest, for one and all made deep obeisance to Raymond as they passed. And now came on the courtiers, bearing aloft the platform on which sat the majestic figure in the pink silk stockings. Raymond began to feel alarmed. If this were (as he more than suspected) his Majesty King Ormund himself, what punishment would be inflicted for the audacious crime of disarming one of his Majesty's bodyguard ? To lose his head was the least he might expect. There could be no doubt that Raymond was alarmed, for he actually forgot to uncover his head in the presence of his sovereign. There he stood, upright and pale, with the spear in his hand, the yellow cap on his head, and his eyes fixed upon the king.

The courtiers saw him. There was a flutter and a murmuring amongst them ; one of them said something to the King, at which he gave a start.

'Now for it!' thought Raymond. He moved his head a little—perhaps he would not have the power of moving it much longer. He wondered how it would look when it was off his shoulders.

The King now leaned forward in his ivory chair and gazed at Raymond intently. Then he gave an order to those about him, and the platform was lowered to the ground by those who carried it. The King stepped from it and came straight towards Raymond, the crowd falling back on either side. How strange! instead of frowning his Majesty wore a very cordial smile. He was close up to Raymond now ; he was throwing his royal arms about his neck ; he was kissing him heartily on both cheeks; he was saying, ‘It delights our heart to see thee. Welcome— welcome to England!’

‘What, in the name of wonder, is the meaning of it all?’ said Raymond to himself.

CHAPTER V.

WHEN it became evident that King Ormund, instead of cutting off Raymond's head, was treating him like a younger brother, Raymond began to pluck up spirit. 'Possibly I look like some friend of his,' he thought; and he resolved to make the most of the mistake, keeping his eyes open for the first chance of escape.

Meanwhile the King overwhelmed him with attentions, and even insisted upon his sitting beside him in the ivory chair; and the courtiers who had to carry this double weight, instead of looking discontented, smiled as if Raymond had been loading them with benefits instead of with himself. The procession now swept onward, and the King himself had hardly more honour than the washerwoman's son. In his wildest dreams

Raymond had never anticipated making such a brilliant entry into London as this.

And had he given up the idea of going back to Honeymead ? Yes ; and he had almost forgotten that there was such a place. The Brindled Cow and Rosamund were like visions of the past which did not much concern him. His yellow cap was the thing that most troubled him, for it pained his head badly. If he had been alone he would have taken it off; but in such fine company he was unwilling to be seen without the handsomest part of his attire.

All this time the King had been talking to him in the most confidential and familiar way imaginable.

'My dear fellow,' he said, 'your arrival is most timely. To-morrow would have been too late. It is most kind of you.'

'I rejoice to be of service——'

'Service, my friend! Such a word between you and me? Never! Counsel—support—sympathy—such as one potentate may claim from another—these I expect from you. But let me explain to you exactly how the case stands. In the first place, I feel that I am getting old.'

After saying this the King paused as if for a reply.   Raymond had never known what it was to pay a compliment in his life; but now something prompted him to say, with a smile and a bow—

'Not at all.   Your Majesty is, to all intents and purposes, as young as I am.'

'Ah, it is very good of you to say that,' sighed his Majesty, looking highly gratified. 'But I really am old—older than you would. suppose; and, if you can believe it, some of my scoundrelly subjects have said (behind my back) that I am growing senile—that is the word the villains use—and they are plotting to dethrone me at ten o'clock to-morrow morning.'

'A conspiracy?'

'Nothing less.   It is announced to take place at Drury Lane Theatre, and the house is sold, from pit to gallery.'

'Oh! it is only a play, then?' said Raymond, in a relieved tone.

'I don't know what you mean by a play,' returned the King, looking slightly hurt.   'It takes place on the stage, of course; but it is as much earnest as anything that goes on in London.'

'Certainly—of course,' said Raymond, anxious not to seem ignorant of fashionable customs. 'But whom do the conspirators mean to put on the throne in your stead? Your son?'

'My Assimund, you mean? Well, that is just the point. My son Assimund is a perfectly harmless young fellow, but—in fact —he is rather too much so.'

'Too much so?'

'Yes—he is—as I might say—hum!' And the King tapped his forehead significantly.

'You don't mean——' And Raymond laid his forefinger between his eyes and then shook it in the air.

'Fact, I assure you.'

'Dear me, how sad!'

'So now you see what I am driving at,' added the King more briskly.

'Well, I hardly—that is——'

'Briefly, then, the part of the usurper has not yet been given out. But I have reigned fifty years, and, between you and me, I'm tired of it. This crown of mine'—the King laid his hand upon the diadem he wore—'often gives me a headache. Ah, I see you understand that. You've felt the same yourself?'

'Why, something of the sort, I confess,' said Raymond, settling his yellow cap on his brow.

'Bless you! what monarch has not? But you are young and hearty—you can stand it. So here is my plan: I decline to submit to force, because the precedent would be dangerous; but I am willing to abdicate. That is my counter-move—my rival attraction, as the stage manager would say. But, if it is to succeed, there is no time to be lost; the posters must be got out at once.'

'Yes, I agree with you,' said Raymond, who was now quite bewildered.

'I was sure I might count on your aid. It is settled, then. As soon as we reach town I will arrange with the advertising agent that your name shall appear upon the bills as my successor in the largest type.'

'I?' cried Raymond, jumping up, and almost oversetting the ivory chair.

'Bless me! what's the matter? Who else but you?'

Raymond sat down again quite dumbfoundered. He a king! It had been the ambition of his life, but now that it was so near being realised he found himself unprepared. Some kinds of good luck are better to look forward to than to have. However, since it seemed inevitable, Raymond was bound to put a good face upon it. Probably he would have a prime minister to give him some hints at starting.

'I shall be happy to make myself of use,' he said politely. 'But I must tell you that it is some time since I governed a kingdom, and I may be a little out of practice.'

'Oh, never mind that,' returned the King, stroking his beard. 'In an absolute monarchy like this the sovereign is responsible to no one. Do as you like; it saves trouble and expense too.'

Raymond smiled, and tried to look at ease. But he resolved to make one more effort to get time for looking about him.

'It will not be best, I suppose, to enter upon my duties at once?' he said. 'The people will have to accustom themselves to the change, and——'

'Nothing of the sort,' interrupted the King. 'I don't believe in too much playing to the pit and gallery, especially when the stalls are inclined to be disorderly. Make your hit with the executioner's axe, if need be.

Don't mince matters—it is better to mince *them.*'

'But are you really so willing to part with your crown? It looks quite as comfortable as my cap feels,' sighed Raymond. They were now within sight of the city gates, and he was feeling rather nervous.

'Do you think so? Suppose you try it on?' said the good-natured monarch, taking his crown off. 'Come, off with your cap!'

Raymond doffed his cap, thrust it into the front of his doublet, and put out his hands to take the crown which the King held towards him.

But as he did so he noticed a singular change come over his Majesty's heretofore jolly visage. The eyes of the venerable potentate opened wider and wider until they were broader than they were long; his forehead wrinkled, and his nostrils expanded. His face from red became crimson, and from crimson purple; and he shook all over.

'Who are you, fellow?' he roared out in a terrible voice. 'How did you get up here? Ho! guards! seize this insolent varlet and cut off his head this moment!'

There was no time to think twice. Ray-

E

mond sprang to his feet, overturning the ivory chair as he did so, so that his transparent Majesty King Ormund fell off to the platform, which trembled at the shock. The fifty courtiers who supported it staggered and lost their footing, and the whole affair came to the ground with a tremendous crash, landing the King in a mud-puddle, and splashing his transparent stockings all over with mire.

Taking advantage of the dismay and confusion thus brought about, Raymond dodged between the legs of a gigantic guard who was on the point of clutching him, butted his head into the stomach of a second, who in falling upset a third, over whom a fourth and fifth stumbled ; and, having by this time got to the brink of the broad and deep ditch beside the road, he crossed it with a flying leap, plunged into the bushes on the further side, and made such good use of his legs that in two or three minutes he was beyond the reach of pursuit.

CHAPTER VI.

DONKEY-BACK.

RAYMOND ran on without paying attention to
the way he was going so long as it was away
from King Ormund and his company. By
and by he came to another road, narrower
than the one he had left, but leading also towards the city. There was a heap of stones
on the roadside, and on this Raymond sat
down to think over his adventure.

It was a puzzle, whichever way he looked
at it. Had the King been making game of
him all along? No, his Majesty had without
doubt looked upon him as a person of consequence. But if so, what had so suddenly un-
deceived him?

'The dwarf must be at the bottom of it,'
said Raymond to himself.

But how? The dwarf had given him the
cap and promised him the kingdom. He had
been very near getting the kingdom; but the

cap had only given him a headache. He pulled it out of his doublet and looked at it.

Yes, it was a fine cap. But Raymond had got to feel such a dislike of it that, had he owned another, he would have thrown this away. But it would never do to make his entrance into London bareheaded.

'But why should I go to London at all?' Raymond asked himself. 'I don't really want to be a king: I only like to think about being one. Shall I go back to the Brindled Cow and Rosamund? Yes, I will!' And with that he got up, put on his cap, and took two or three steps in the direction of Honeymead.

'But what an ass I should be,' he said, stopping short, 'to turn back at the very gates of London! Besides, it is too late to get back to Honeymead to-night. I won't return before to-morrow. Something may happen after all.'

He faced about once more towards London.

'It is an odd thing,' he remarked to himself as he went along, 'how I keep changing my mind first one way and then another. Why is it? It used not to be so when I was in Honeymead. It almost seems as if I were not the same fellow; or as if I were sometimes myself, and sometimes somebody else. I believe there must be something of that kind the matter with me,' he continued after a while. 'Look how those courtiers treated me. They were all cap and knee to me one moment, and the next they were all shouting out "Who is he? Cap and knee—who is he?" Hullo! I have an idea! It is—it isn't. —can it be—the cap?'

He snatched it off his head, and round the band he read again the couplet that had mystified him before :—

> Cap on—cap and knee !
> Cap off—who is he?

The words began to have a meaning now. Fairies and magic spells were at that time common-place matters in England. Fairy stories were not written then, but the events they tell about used to happen. The dwarf himself had called the cap a talisman. 'I will try the experiment with the next person I see,' said Raymond to himself.

The words were scarcely out of his mouth when a noise of pattering hoofs made him

look round, and he saw a young fellow riding
towards him on the extreme end of a small
donkey. Raymond stood in the middle of
the road, his cap in his hand.

'Get out of the way, you!' called out the
rider as he drew near. 'I'm going to the
Seven Brethren. Now then, stupid!'

'I also am in a hurry to get to London,'
said Raymond politely. 'Couldn't you give
me a ride there?'

'Mind your eye, numskull!' cried the
other; and he tried to drive his donkey
directly over Raymond. But Raymond
caught the bridle, and at the same time
put on his cap. Everything depended on
what the donkey-rider did next.

Greatly to Raymond's gratification—
though it half-frightened him too—the fellow
immediately slipped backwards over his donkey's tail; and, having reached the ground,
made an awkward but obsequious salute.

'Beg your Worship's pardon humbly!'
said he, ducking his head and scraping his
foot at every few words. 'Didn't know your
Worship at first. Hope your Worship will
pardon a poor lad whose intellects are not
quite right.'

Indeed, the fellow appeared only half-witted. He had round goggle eyes, a silly mouth, and scarcely any forehead at all.

As for Raymond he felt more like hugging the fellow than merely pardoning him; but he remembered that he must keep up his dignity. Moreover, he now perceived that the wearing of the cap made almost as much change in his own feelings as in other people's opinion of him.

'I will overlook your mistake,' he said condescendingly; 'and in proof of it I will make use of your donkey as far as the city; for I am weary, and there is not much time to lose.'

'Indeed, then, your Worship, he's not fit for a gentleman like your Worship to be riding on,' replied the fellow, ducking again; 'but, if your Worship doesn't mind, I should be proud to see your Worship sitting on him; and he'll carry your Worship well.'

Raymond mounted accordingly, and the party proceeded on their way, the fellow trotting behind, and occasionally persuading the donkey with the oaken cudgel he carried. Meanwhile Raymond asked him some questions.

'You are going to the Seven Brethren?'

'Yes, your Worship. There are good things there, as your Worship knows.'

'How should I know?'

'La! as if I couldn't see that your Worship was one of them himself!'

'It must be the same Seven Brethren of which the dwarf spoke,' thought Raymond; and he said aloud, 'They meet to-night at five o'clock, I think?'

'Right, your Worship. And your Worship may trust me. "Yellow-cap" is the password, "seven" the number, and "five" the time. Isn't it, your Worship?'

Raymond felt much obliged by this information, though he was careful not to say so. When they came to the city gates he slipped off the donkey at a moment when the other was not looking, at the same time removing his cap; when he had the pleasure of seeing the fellow turn to him and ask him whether he had seen 'his Worship?' Raymond only shook his head in reply; and then, following the donkey and its owner at a distance, he presently saw them turn into a narrow archway.

CHAPTER VII.

THE DARK PASSAGE.

RAYMOND crossed over to the opposite side of the road, in order to take a look at the house to which the archway belonged. It was a little old-fashioned inn, squeezed in between two tall houses, like a shabby dwarf between two respectable giants. Over the door hung a sign—a painting of a man with seven heads. They were ugly faces, all of them, each with its peculiar kind of ugliness, and Raymond felt a separate kind of dislike towards each one. Nevertheless (as might have been expected, seeing that there was but one body between them) they bore a sort of family likeness one to another. 'That must be a very wicked body,' Raymond thought; 'it must be capable of committing all the seven deadly sins at once.' It was thick and shapeless, with short crooked legs, and very long arms. Underneath was written, ' *The Seven Brethren.*'

As he stood in the shadow on the opposite side of the street, with his cap under his arm, Raymond felt half-minded not to enter the inn which hung out so uninviting a sign. How different were these faces from those of Armand, Dorimund, Sigismund, and the rest of the rosy young farmers who drank milk at the Brindled Cow! Should he go back there even now? There he would be sure of a welcome: he was not sure of a welcome here. Raymond hesitated. But before he could make up his mind the barmaid of the Seven Brethren appeared at the door of the inn. She soon espied him where he stood, and smiled and beckoned to him.

'Come over, come over, my lad,' she said ; ' it's just upon supper-time, and there's a chop on the gridiron, and a draught of brown ale I'll draw for you. Come ; you look right hungry.'

Her voice and look made Raymond's heart beat, for, in a certain way, they were like Rosamund's. And yet they were unlike. She had eyes like Rosamund's, but the expression in them was one which Rosamund never wore. Her manner of speaking, too, resembled Rosamund's. Yet Rosamund had never spoken in quite that tone. Raymond hardly knew whether to be pleased or shocked. After a little hesitation he put on his cap and came across the street to her.

'Oh! my Lord, I'm sure I crave your pardon!' exclaimed the girl, dropping him a curtsey. But though her words were humble Raymond fancied he saw a mischievous sparkle in her eye which made him suspect that she might be making fun of him. 'I didn't recognise your Lordship in the shadow over there,' she continued, in a still softer voice. 'They have been expecting your Lordship.'

Now that Raymond was close to the girl she seemed much prettier than before. 'What is your name?' he asked her.

'Silvia, please your Lordship.'

'Silvia—not Rosamund?'

'Oh, no, please your Lordship. Rosamund is such a vulgar name.'

'You are very pretty, Silvia.'

'Your Lordship is very good to say so,' replied she, casting down her sparkling eyes and curtseying again.

'What is that round your neck, Silvia?'

'That is the half of a brass farthing, please your Lordship, that I and my lover split between us this afternoon.'

'I thought it was the half of a spade guinea.'

'I'd be glad to exchange it for that,' said Silvia, looking up, with a smile.

'Would you exchange your lover at the same time?'

'If the other was a handsome man,' said she, with a coquettish glance. 'But won't your Lordship come in? It's past five, I'm sure.'

'I will follow you,' said he. And they went in.

'Will your Lordship take my hand?' she said. 'The passage is very dark and winding.' She put her hand in his as she spoke.

'Why is there no light here?' he asked.

'This passage can never be lighted, please your Lordship: the goblins pinch out the wick of the candle with their fingers.'

'Are there goblins here?' said Raymond, drawing back.

'Keep hold of my hand, and they will do your Lordship no harm.'

'Does this passage belong to them?'

'Mind the steps, please your Lordship,'
said Silvia suddenly. 'If you were to lose
me here you would never see light again.'

'How strange your voice sounds! Are
you Silvia?'

'I am not Rosamund, at any rate!' replied his conductor, with a low laugh. 'It's
the vault of the passage makes my voice
sound hoarse.'

'We must be a long way underground.
And this darkness is like a block of black
marble. And I feel as if creatures were
walking around me who can see me though
I cannot see them.'

'Their eyes are more used to the darkness
than your Lordship's.'

'How far have we still to go?'

'Not far. I shall leave your Lordship at
the next corner.'

'What am I to do then?'

No reply was made to this question. But
in a few moments Raymond lost his hold of
the hand that had guided him, and a voice
said, in a whining tone—

'Won't your Lordship spare me a trifle
for coming so far?'

'I—I'm afraid I have nothing to give,'

said Raymond, putting his hand in his empty pocket.

'A kiss is all I want from your Lordship,' answered the voice; and then a pair of lips met Raymond's in the darkness. The lips were cold as ice, but the breath that came between them was hot as flame.

Then all was silence. Had Raymond kissed one of the invisible goblins instead of Silvia? Or was Silvia herself a goblin?

Be that as it might Raymond was left in an awkward situation. For all he knew he was in the middle of an underground laby-rinth; and the next step might land him at the bottom of some pitfall. Raymond remembered that long ago, when he was a small boy, his mother had once shut him up in the dark closet behind the kitchen chimney, because he had made a mud-pie on the ironing-board. That closet had seemed black enough, but what was it compared with this? Besides, Rosamund had come after a while and secretly let him out, and they had spent the afternoon together in the barn. But Rosamund could never come to him here; and that goblin kiss upon his lips had taken away his right to hope for her.

While these thoughts had been passing through his mind he had been slowly feeling his way forward; but all at once he was brought to a stand by a sharp prick on the breast as if from the point of a levelled spear.

'Who comes?' said a harsh voice.

'Only me,' replied Raymond in his most conciliating tone.

'Have you the password?' demanded the voice again.

Recollecting what the donkey-driver had told him, Raymond answered at a venture—

'Yellow-cap!'

'Pass on, Yellow-cap!' said the voice.

He passed on, hoping that his wanderings were now to end. But after a few steps he felt against his throat the smooth sharp edge of a sword, which caused him to start back with a cry.

'Who comes?' said a snarling voice.

'Yellow-cap!' Raymond replied.

'The number, Yellow-cap?'

'Seven!' hazarded Raymond.

'Pass on, Seven!' said the voice.

Raymond stepped forward nervously, stumbled down an unexpected pair of steps, and all in a moment there was a brilliant dazzle of light close to his eyes. It vanished as suddenly as it came; but it had given him a fleeting impression of many grisly faces pressing around him on all sides, with fire-lit eyes all fixed upon his. On the succeeding darkness, which seemed more intense than ever, the image of these faces was still somehow discernible; while from amidst them came a hissing voice, which said—

'Who comes?'

'Yellow-cap!'

'The number?'

'Seven!'

'The time?'

'Five!'

'Pass!' said the voice.

And immediately (though how it happened he could not tell) Raymond found himself in a square, low-ceilinged, comfortable room, with a large lamp burning in the centre of the table, around which were seated six men, each with a long pipe in his mouth and a tankard of ale before him.

CHAPTER VIII.

THE MAGIC EYE.

THE six men arose, and each in turn, and then all together, uttered the words—

'Welcome, Yellow-cap!'

Then he among them who had the biggest nose and the most sweeping moustachios came forward, made Raymond a grave salute, and, taking him by the arm, led him to a chair at the head of the table.

'The tale of the Seven Brethren is at last complete,' said he.

'Hear! hear!' gruffly responded the others.

'Brother Yellow-cap,' continued the first speaker, 'let me introduce you to our Brotherhood. I am the Prime Maniac. He on your right is the Chancellor of the Jingle. Next to him is the Home Doggerel. At the foot of the table is the First Lord of the Seesaw. The Foreign Doggerel is next on the left.

F

Next again the Lord Privy Gander. One and all of us are bound to aid you, abet you, and obey you, so long as you own and wear the yellow cap. Once more, welcome, Yellow-cap!'

'Welcome!' chimed in the Brethren; and they raised their tankards to their lips and emptied them at a draught.

'We do not call one another by our titles,' said the Lord Privy Gander.

'Nor by our names,' added the Chancellor of the Jingle.

'Nor by our surnames,' pursued the Home Doggerel.

'But by our nicknames,' observed the Foreign Doggerel.

'By the mystic syllables repeated,' said the First Lord of the Seesaw.

Hereupon a curious ceremony took place. Beginning with the Lord Privy Gander, and so on in regular order to the First Lord of the Seesaw, each brother in rapid succession spoke his own nickname, with the following result.

'Ruba!' said the Lord Privy Gander.

'Dubb!' said the Chancellor of the Jingle.

'Dubsix!' said the Home Doggerel.

'Menin!' said the Foreign Doggerel.

'Atub!' said the First Lord of the See-saw.

'Gyp is my nickname,' remarked the Prime Maniac, 'because the verse had not feet enough to go all round. Did you ever hear anything like this before?'

'I fancied at one moment that I had; but now I don't know,' Yellow-cap answered.

'There is only one inconvenience about it,' observed Ruba.

'We must always speak in order,' added Dubb.

'On pain of spoiling our metre,' put in Dubsix.

'And our rhyme,' continued Menin.

'Except Gyp,' added Atub, 'who can talk when he likes, and that is his chief advantage.'

'It is an advantage in more ways than one,' Gyp remarked. 'Not only can I talk when I like, but none of the others can say anything unless all the rest are willing; because his speaking makes it necessary that all the rest should have something to say, and that Ruba should begin. The only laws that we recognise are metrical laws, and they, as you know, are the strictest in the world.'

Yellow-cap felt rather bewildered ; but he was glad to find that he himself was not included in the metrical system. Some error in either rhyme or rhythm would, he felt sure, have been the consequence.

'Let me order you a pipe and tankard,' continued Gyp, ringing the bell. Somewhat to Yellow-cap's surprise Silvia appeared at the door in answer to the summons. The pipe and the tankard were soon brought ; and the new-comer's health having then been drunk in ceremonious silence, the formal part of his reception seemed to be at an end.

Meanwhile he had improved such opportunity as he had had for examining the faces about him, and was not altogether astonished to find that they were the originals of the many-headed portrait on the inn signboard. Only the seventh (and central) head, the ugliest of all, was missing ; the Brethren, exclusive of himself, being only six in number. Beer-drinking and tobacco-smoking seemed to be the business of the meeting. Yellow-cap had never until this evening drunk any-

thing stronger than milk or smoked anything
more dangerous than sweet-fern; but the
beer gave him courage for the tobacco, and
he soon began to feel at home.

'But can you tell me how I got here?'
he inquired of Gyp, who sat nearest him, and
who, moreover, could answer without setting
all the feet running. 'The way was long
and perilous and as black as pitch; and .
yet, when the door was open just now, I
could see right through the house into the
street, and it did not seem more than
twelve paces.'

'Did you come alone?' asked Gyp, puffing a long whiff of smoke up towards the
ceiling.

'Alone with Silvia.'

'Ah-h-h! Silvia sometimes leads the best
of men astray. But you got here at last, and
that is more than many do. And you were
but just in time. The King prints his placards
to-night.'

'What placards?' asked Yellow-cap in-
nocently.

'Announcing his "successor"—a farce in
one act.'

'And who is his successor?'

'Who would you like him to be?' inquired Gyp, smiling.

At this all the Brethren looked at one another and winked mysteriously. Yellow-cap, who was fast becoming wise, and who knew more about this matter than he cared to admit, could not help wondering at his queer position—the Head of a Secret Society hostile to the very monarch who had offered him his kingdom that same afternoon. The thought of it made him feel quite hot; and he was so far forgetting himself as to be on the point of taking off his cap to cool his forehead, when Gyp caught his arm, and a murmur of horror ran through the assembly.

'Forbear! as you value your credit!' cried Ruba.

'And your gentility!' exclaimed Dubb.

'And your influence!' called out Dubsix.

'And your success!' shouted Menin.

'And your reputation!' bawled Atub.

'It is against the first law of the Brotherhood,' added Ruba.

'We all have headaches,' asserted Dubb.

'We couldn't live without them,' declared Dubsix.

'Would you commit suicide?' demanded Menin.

'Be guilty of treason?' hiccoughed Atub, who had swallowed some smoke the wrong way.

'Good gracious!' was all that poor Yellow-cap was able to reply.

'Allow me to explain,' interposed Gyp courteously. 'The Seven Brethren are the outcome of an artificial civilisation. It is our strength and also our weakness that we never seem to be what we are. Our laws are binding because they are irrational. Our power is great because it is an imposition. Our respectability is perfect because it is a fraud. We gain our ends because our ends are ourselves. Our union is strong because it depends on mutual distrust. In a word, we are the Everlasting Unreality! Have you understood me?'

'Not in the least,' replied Yellow-cap.

''Tis well. No one of us understands either himself or his brother. He who understands or is understood is anathema.'

'Dear me!' ejaculated Yellow-cap.

'You have heard of the cap of invisibility?'

' I believe so.'

' The yellow cap is more wondrous yet
—it is only when you put it on that you
can be seen—at all events by the world.'

'Dear me!' ejaculated Yellow-cap again.

Hereupon all the Brethren twisted their
moustachios, knocked the ashes out of their
pipes, refilled them, lighted them, and smoked
in silence.

' By the way,' said Yellow-cap at length,
' about the signboard outside the inn-door.
I recognise six of the portraits, but where is
the seventh ? He was the one whose face
was the most ugly and disagreeable of all ;
but I don't see him here.'

' He is here,' said Ruba.

Yellow-cap was going to ask, ' Where ?'
but Gyp laid his hand upon his arm and
whispered in his ear that he must not in-
terrupt until the whole verse had run itself
out.

' We have seen him,' continued Dubb.

' The likeness is good,' pronounced Dubsix.

' Flattering,' affirmed Menin.

' I can think of nothing to say,' confessed
Atub.

'Come and look in our mirror,' said Gyp, taking Yellow-cap by the arm and leading him to the end of the room.

Now, against the wall at this end hung a very odd specimen of a looking-glass. Its surface was convex, and in shape it was neither square, nor round, nor exactly oval, for it was pointed at both ends. Its length was divided into three parts, of which the central one was black, and those at the sides of a dull white like china. Altogether it looked like a gigantic eye plucked from the forehead of some Polyphemus; and hung up in the old inn-parlour, where, if it could no longer see anything itself, it might at least give those who gazed into it a distorted image of themselves.

When Yellow-cap, however, first fixed his eyes upon this curious mirror he could see nothing but a profound depth of blackness; but in the midst of this obscure movements were presently visible. By and by the many wavering shapes grew clearer and drew near to one another and, as it were, melted together, until at last a definite image stood forth against the dark background.

A strange figure it was—of a short-legged,

shapeless man, with no less than seven heads upon his shoulders. Six of these Yellow-cap knew at once; but the seventh—the central and most important one of all—was unknown to him. And what an unpleasant set of features it had, to be sure!

The whole company had gathered behind Yellow-cap, who was standing directly in front of the mirror.

'You don't know him?' spoke the voice of Ruba.

'He knows you,' said Dubb.

'He is an old friend of yours,' remarked Dubsix.

'And a very dear one,' added Menin.

'And a very false one,' observed Atub.

'What does it all mean?' inquired Yellow-cap.

'If you will give yourself the trouble to lay your left finger beside your nose it might inform you,' said Gyp courteously.

Yellow-cap did as he was desired. The reflection in the glass lifted the corresponding finger and laid it beside the nose of no other than the central head.

'Would you mind winking your left eye?' continued Gyp.

Yellow-cap did so. The central head alone winked back.

'Now you might stick out your tongue,' suggested Gyp.

Yellow-cap tried this experiment also: the seventh head was the only one that imitated the gesture.

'This is absurd,' exclaimed Yellow-cap indignantly. 'The central head imitates everything I do; it even pretends to look like me, which is ridiculous, for it is ugly, while I am——'

'Perhaps you have never looked in a mirror before?' said Gyp gently.

'Yes, I have—in tin pans,' returned Yellow-cap warmly.

'Tin pans are untrustworthy,' said Gyp. 'This is the best mirror in the world, and that is the reason why it is in the shape of an eye, without any face belonging to it.'

'I should think you would be the last people in the world to want a good mirror, or any mirror at all!' exclaimed Yellow-cap testily.

'We don't want it—and that is why we have it. We call it our eyesore; and it is the eye of our destiny. Look again.'

'What is this?' muttered Yellow-cap. 'All the heads are melting into one another; now they are all swallowed up in the central head; and now that head looks more like me than ever, and yet uglier; and now— why, it looks like the old dwarf I carried across the river, and—which am I?'

He turned round, and, behold! the six Brethren were seated each one in his place at the table, smoking and drinking as gravely as ever, and looking as if they had never once stirred from their chairs. Glancing back at the mirror, he saw that it had returned to its former unreflecting condition, only a few vanishing shadows being yet visible in its black depths.

'It certainly is different from a tin pan,' thought he as he went back to his chair at the head of the table.

'Nothing more than an optical illusion,' said Gyp, filling Yellow-cap's pipe from his own tobacco-pouch, and handing it to him courteously. 'There is no harm in it—none at all.'

'Especially as it makes you our Head,' observed Ruba.

'I move we suspend the rules,' said Dubb.

'I second that motion,' said Dubsix.

'We mustn't put our feet into our business,' remarked Menin in an explanatory way.

'The only rule we never suspend is the rule that no rule shall not sometimes be suspended,' added Atub.

'So be it,' said Gyp agreeably. 'The metrical system is hereby suspended for the rest of the evening. Have another tankard of ale, Brother Yellow-cap?'

'I don't care if I do—with a Head on it,' returned Yellow-cap, putting an emphasis on the 'Head.' And when the ale was brought he arose, with a frown on his brow, and spoke to them in a bold voice as follows :—

'Yes, I am your Head, for no one of you is so unreal as I. When I was a little boy I sat blowing soap-bubbles, and saw the Appanage of Royalty appear amidst the clouds of the wash-tub. He promised me this cap, and now the cap is mine. I have paid for it all I had in the world, and now I mean to get my profit out of it. You have waited for me : I have never waited for you ; for I could succeed without you ; but, without me, you would be nothing !'

'Hear! hear!' exclaimed the Brethren in chorus, seeming much pleased with Yellow-cap's eloquence.

'Now, Brother Gyp, you may state the object of this meeting,' said Yellow-cap, resuming his seat.

Gyp bowed and pulled a roll of parchment out of Brother Dubsix's pocket, which was written all over with musical notes in the bass and treble clefs.

'The object is a twofold one,' he began.

'I object to that expression,' interrupted Dubb.

'Why?' demanded Gyp in a mortified tone.

'Only for the sake of speaking out of metre,' replied Dubb; at which the Brethren looked at one another and lifted their eyebrows.

'Well, at all events,' said Gyp, recovering his good-humour, 'we want to get the King out and put the usurper in his place.'

'Has anything been done to prepare the people for this change?' inquired Yellow-cap. 'Are they on our side?'

'We've got fifty paid *claqueurs*—I know that,' said Atub.

'And we have suspended the rule about full-dress in the stalls,' added Dubsix.

'Ah!' exclaimed Menin, nodding his head and crossing his feet on the table in republican style, 'there is a great deal in that.'

'How are you going to depose him?' Yellow-cap asked.

'In the usual way,' said Gyp : 'by finding a rhyme to him, and then putting him under foot.'

'But suppose he won't be deposed?'

'Ah, it will be our turn then,' said Ruba gloomily. 'He will appoint a successor, and we shall be repeated backwards.'

At this all the Brethren curled their moustachios and sighed deeply.

'Who is to find the rhyme to "King Ormund?"' inquired Yellow-cap, to whom this affair began to look rather irregular.

'Who but the usurper?' cried all the Brethren together.

'And who is he?' said Yellow-cap.

Hereupon the Brethren one and all took their pipes out of their mouths and deliberately pointed at Yellow-cap with their pipe-stems. At the same time they puffed out a vast cloud of tobacco-smoke, which rose to the ceiling of the room and collected there.

'Do you mean me?' cried Yellow-cap, recoiling. 'I never made a rhyme in my life.'

'You have said it!' they answered with one voice; 'so let it be!'

At this moment they all arose and solemnly emptied their tankards; then they piled the tankards together in the centre of the table; and Dubsix and Atub, taking each an arm of Yellow-cap, raised him from the floor and seated him upon the pile as upon a throne.

The six Brethren now joined hands and began to dance round and round the table, puffing volumes of smoke from their pipes as they went. Faster and wilder moved the dance, thicker and yellower whirled the smoke-wreaths, and the six faces sped dizzily round the table, until it seemed to Yellow-cap as if he were encircled by a great ring of face, with one broad nose, one endless grinning mouth, and a single leering eye in the forehead.

By and by the room began to spin round also—such, at least, was Yellow-cap's impression. Round and round it spun like a teetotum, moving as fast as the dancers did, but in the opposite direction. The smoke, driven together by these contrary motions, was whirled into a sort of hollow dome over Yellow-cap's head. The yellow light from the lamp shone upon that smoky dome, and its shape became defined more and more distinctly, until at last it hung poised in air—a gigantic image of the very yellow cap which Yellow-cap wore.

Gradually it settled down lower and lower, as if to shut him in. He tried to rise from his tankard throne, but a heavy weight from above seemed to prevent him. And now, glaring upon him through the maze of flying phantoms, he saw the mirror of the Brethren, no longer black and lifeless, but fierce and flaming as the eye of a giant demon. And through the centre of that fiery pupil he saw the Brethren, one after another, take a flying leap; not vanishing suddenly, but dwindling away, smaller and smaller, until they could be seen no more. Each as he leaped threw back at Yellow-cap a malicious leer and beckoned to him mockingly to follow. Gyp was the last; and as he sprang Yellow-cap wrenched himself from his throne—which fell behind him with a crash—and strove to follow.

But the yellow cap of stifling smoke came down upon him and shut him in. He sank downwards, choking and gasping; and he heard, ringing through the heated air, a sound of laughter that reminded him of Silvia.

CHAPTER IX.

ON THE STAGE.

YELLOW-CAP opened his eyes, which felt dry and hot. It was indeed Silvia, who was laughing, and bidding him wake up, for it was past eight o'clock in the morning. And where had Yellow-cap passed the night? Underneath the table in the inn parlour, where that extraordinary meeting of the Seven Brethren had taken place. As Yellow-cap got slowly to his feet he pressed both hands to his head, which felt like a newly-roasted chestnut, with the kernel loose inside; but the yellow cap was still fast about his brows. He longed to take it off and put his head under the pump; but that luxury, he knew, was now and hereafter forbidden him.

'Where are the other fellows?' he asked, turning to Silvia. 'They jumped through the fiery eye——'

G 2

'Through what, your Lordship?' cried Silvia, opening her eyes very wide.

'Through that,' said Yellow-cap, pointing to the end of the room where the mysterious mirror hung. But, to his great perplexity, there was to be seen there only a very common-place old looking-glass, made in three compartments, and mounted in a tarnished frame. In the light of the morning sun, which was pouring through the dusty window-panes, it looked not at all like an eye, and it was absurd to suppose that anybody could have jumped through it.

'Things always look so different in the morning,' remarked Silvia good-humouredly. ' But, if it please your Lordship, I am sent by the Brethren to say that they are waiting for you in the front room.'

Yellow-cap felt not at all in the mood to lead a conspiracy; but still he tried to put a good face upon the matter. 'Lead on!' said he ; and Silvia opened the door and went before him across a small enclosed yard to another door, on which she tapped; and Yellow-cap, passing in, found himself once more in the presence of his six friends. They were eating devilled bones, and were dressed

in long white dominoes. Each had a play-
book beside his plate, and they were apparently studying their parts for the morning
performance.

'Good morning! Fine day for the depo-
sition,' said Gyp, acting as spokesman for the
rest. 'Have a bone?'

'I have no appetite,' replied Yellow-cap.
'Why are you all dressed in white?'

'So that we may be the blacker inside,'
said Ruba, looking up from his book.

'It is the court-dress of conspirators,'
added Dubb.

'We are clothed in the unwritten pages
of history,' continued Dubsix.

'We shall be red hereafter,' said Menin,
archly.

'Because we rose against the tyrant,' con-
cluded Atub, with a sigh.

'They are apt to be rather stupid at this
hour in the morning,' remarked Gyp, turning to Yellow-cap, 'but they will get warmed
to it presently. May I ask whether you are
perfect in your part?'

'I have not thought of any rhyme to
"Ormund,"' said Yellow-cap.

'Any rhyme will do,' Gyp went on; 'and

perhaps the Home or the Foreign Doggerel
will be able to help you to one when the
time comes.'

'Brethren,' said Yellow-cap, clearing his
throat, 'I propose we put off this affair until
to-morrow.   I don't feel at all well this
morning ; and besides, a thing like this ought
to be done after dark, not in broad daylight.'

Hereupon the six Brethren looked at one
another and gave a low whistle ; and after a
pause Gyp said—

'This day is the only day in the year on
which conspiracies are allowed to take place,
and they are not permitted later than ten
o'clock in the forenoon.   But I may mention
that the theatre is always darkened, and is
lighted by artificial means.'

'I do not understand,' said Yellow-cap,
'how a conspiracy can succeed, if the people
who are conspired against fix the time when
it is to come off.'

'What sort of an audience should we get,'
replied Gyp, 'if the date of the performance
was not advertised beforehand ?   We should
find ourselves playing to empty boxes.   Besides, conspiracies are costly ; and if——'

'If you please,' said Silvia, opening the

door, 'it is just upon nine o'clock, and the donkey waits.'

'We come!' said all the Brethren together, They rose up, put their play-books in their pockets, and joining hands so as to form a circle, with Gyp and Yellow-cap in the middle of it, they rapidly repeated five times over the following mystic chant, Gyp beating time for them with the forefinger of his right hand on the five fingers of his left :—

Ruba—Dubb—Dubsix—Menin—Atub—Chorus—Gyp !

This having been duly performed, Gyp, with an air of great respect, took Yellow-cap by the arm and led him out to the street, the other five Brethren following behind. Yellow-cap, who had by this time almost ceased feeling surprised at anything, did not find it especially wonderful that the donkey which was in waiting was the same on which he had ridden the evening before, and that its driver was the same half-witted youth who had given him such useful information about the passwords. This youth grinned and ducked his head when he saw Yellow-cap, and held the stirrup for him to mount.

As Yellow-cap did so the thought occurred to him that perhaps he might get a chance to gallop away down some side-street, and so make his escape even at the last moment; for it must be confessed that he did not feel much courage for this adventure.   Much to his disappointment, however, no sooner was he in the saddle than the donkey-driver took hold of the donkey's bridle on one side and Silvia on the other ; and in this way they set out.

'Why are you coming with us, Silvia ?' Yellow-cap asked, after they had gone a little way. 'Are you one of the conspirators ?'

'No, your Lordship, not exactly,' she replied ; 'but I usually take the part of Columbine, and sometimes lead the ballet.'

'So it's to be a pantomime, is it ?' thought Yellow-cap. 'I wonder what the grand transformation scene will be like ?'

Then he turned to the donkey-driver, who was plodding along with a vacant grin upon his features, and asked him what part he had to play.

'Oh, please your Worship,' he replied, 'I'm to be the Clown ; and that young woman,' pointing to Silvia, 'is to be my sweetheart, if I can catch her.'

'And I'm to be Harlequin, I suppose,'

said Yellow-cap to himself. 'Well, I'm sure I begin to feel like one.'

Meanwhile they had entered the chief street of the town, which led to the Drury Lane Theatre. This was a handsome building of white marble, with columns and a sculptured frieze; it was the model which the Greeks long afterwards followed when they built their Parthenon. A great multitude of people were collected in front of the pit and gallery entrances; and when they caught sight of Yellow-cap they set up a great buzzing and murmuring, mingled with shouts and huzzas and waving of hats and handkerchiefs.

'There he is! that's him!' cried the people one to another. 'That's him on the grey charger, with the captive prince and princess a-leading of him along. Oh, ain't he a swell!'

'Hurry up, guv'nor, or you'll be late!' shouted others; and indeed as Yellow-cap looked up at the clock which was placed in the pediment of the theatre he saw that it marked five minutes to ten.

'Hadn't we better move a little faster?' he said anxiously to Silvia. 'And how are we ever to get through all this crowd?'

'Oh, we have time enough,' she answered very unconcernedly. 'And, since we must go in by the stage-door, the crowd won't hinder us.'

As she spoke they turned down a narrow alley to the left, and soon came to a small entrance in the side of the building. Through this the donkey quietly walked, and up a flight of steps to an inner passageway. Before he knew where he was Yellow-cap found himself on an immense stage, at the further side of which was standing King Ormund himself, surrounded by a group of courtiers. The courtiers were all enveloped in long white dominoes, the sight of which caused Yellow-cap to look behind him with a sudden misgiving. He had supposed until this moment that the six Brethren were following behind him; but he now discovered that, except for Silvia and the half-witted donkey-driver, he was quite alone.

'What has become of them?' he cried in dismay.

'There they are,' said Silvia coolly, pointing to the group of courtiers. 'Where else should they be?'

'They have deserted me, then?'

'Not at all; but as the conspiracy is all

on your account it is only fair that you should take all the risks. If the conspiracy were to fail, and they were to have their heads cut off, there could be no conspiracy next year ; but if only you are executed your cap would be saved, and there would be no difficulty about finding some one else to wear it.'

'Upon my word,' muttered Yellow-cap to himself rather angrily, 'however this matter goes I am resolved that I will not lose my head before making those six rascals shake in their shoes. Courtiers indeed! We shall see.'

At this moment the curtain drew up and showed the vast audience crowding every part of the theatre. A great clapping of hands and stamping of feet followed, and there were several catcalls and whistlings from the pit and gallery. Almost every member of the audience was provided with a programme headed, '*Grand Annual Panto-mime: the Conspiracy*,' and containing a list of the performers. Attendants were also moving about hawking librettos of the dialogue. Familiar though Yellow-cap had become with marvels, he could not help wondering how anybody could know what he was going to say. He certainly did not know himself.

The audience had now become silent— not a sound was to be heard in the theatre except the occasional rustle of a programme. Yellow-cap dismounted from his donkey, which remained on the stage in the care of the driver, and walked towards the King. His Majesty was eyeing him very closely. The great clock outside the building struck ten. The King and Yellow-cap saluted each other, and Yellow-cap said—

'I hope I have not kept your Majesty waiting.'

'Not at all,' the monarch replied. 'But, stay! surely I cannot be mistaken. Are not you the gallant prince whom I had the plea- sure of meeting yesterday, and who vanished so strangely just when we were about to ex- change hats?'

'Your Majesty's memory is not at fault,' Yellow-cap answered.

'Bless my soul! my dear fellow,' the King exclaimed with much heartiness, 'allow me to give you a hug!'

At this there was a great outburst of ap- plause from the audience, which his Majesty acknowledged by bowing and smiling. After it was over he continued—

'And now tell me, where on earth did you vanish to? I could have sworn you were beside me—when, almost while I was looking at you, you were gone; and in your place was a dirty, impertinent varlet who tried to snatch my crown out of my very hands.'

'Indeed. An audacious fellow, truly!'

'Ah, but he got his deserts. Ha! I flatter myself he will never again try *that* game. No, by my faith!'

'What did you do to him?'

'I grappled with him, and, after a tremendous struggle, I managed to get him by the throat and bowed him backwards to the earth. I say "to the earth," because the villains who should have upheld my platform had let it fall. Never mind—I had all their heads before supper-time.'

'And the robber?'

'There was not much left of him,' replied his Majesty, with a hearty laugh. 'After I had strangled him I flung his carcass to my retainers, who made mincemeat of it in no time. But all this is by the way. You have not told me what became of you.'

Now, Yellow-cap had a good imagination ;
and seeing that the King had made up a clever
story, he resolved to do his best to tell another
as good.

'Your Majesty must know,' he said, 'that
among my other modest gifts I include that
of making myself invisible at pleasure and
transporting myself to distant places by the
force of a wish.   Just at the moment when
we were about to exchange hats I happened
to remember that I had important business
elsewhere ; and since I had a long way to go,
and very little time to go in, I was obliged to
leave your Majesty without ceremony.   But,
as you see, I have lost no time in again pre-
senting myself before you.'

There was a round of applause at this
speech, but neither so long nor so loud as at
that of the King.

'I hope we may not again be parted,' said
his Majesty graciously.   'In fact, I really
don't know what I should have done without you.'

Here Yellow-cap felt a gentle pull at
his sleeve, and looking round he saw that
Silvia was holding out to him a small slip
of paper.   He took it from her, and read the

following words which had been written upon
it :—

'A rhyme to King Ormund.'

The King had noticed this transaction,
and immediately asked—

'What have you got there ?'

'A rhyme to King Ormund,' replied
Yellow-cap, repeating the words which he
had read without thinking of the effect they
might have upon his hearer. But the audience took the point immediately, and the
clapping of hands and stamping were this
time both loud and long.

And now something happened which
Yellow-cap could not at first understand.
The King hummed-and-hah'ed and looked
rather embarrassed, but said nothing, and by
and by began searching in his pockets as if
he had mislaid something. The audience
saw that something was wrong, and catcalls
and whistling and impertinent remarks were
heard from all parts of the house. The King
turned red, and stood first on one foot and
then on another ; and at last he muttered
between his teeth—

'I'll have that prompter's head cut off!'

'If your Majesty will allow me, said

Silvia, coming forward, 'I can tell you what comes next.' And she whispered a few words in his ear.

'Ah! of course—of course!' exclaimed the King, looking much relieved. 'I have had hardly any time to study my part; and I hope,' he added, turning to the audience, 'that you will excuse me.' 'Go it, old boy!' sang out somebody from the gallery. The King pulled down his ruffles and went on.

'"A rhyme to King Ormund, eh?" Dear me! Then you are one of the conspirators?'

'I have that honour,' replied Yellow-cap. 'In fact, I am the chief of them; and I can, if you like, tell you the names of the others,' he added, glancing at the Prime Maniac and his companions.

'You must not say that,' said Silvia in a low voice, twitching his sleeve again; 'it isn't in your part.'

'I shall take my own part,' returned Yellow-cap, loud enough to be heard all over the theatre, 'and do what I like with it.'

'That's the talk!' called out a man from the pit. 'Give it 'em, youngster, and we'll see fair play.'

'Well, you have got the best of me,' said

the King, shrugging his shoulders good-humouredly, 'and I have only one regret.'

'What may that be?' Yellow-cap inquired.

'Only that, since you *have* got the best of me, I am prevented from enjoying the pleasure I had looked forward to of making you my successor. But, after all, it comes to the same thing in the end—for you, at any rate. And things being as they are, of course they could not be otherwise. Come—despatch!' And so saying the venerable monarch wrapped his mantle round his head and struck an heroic attitude.

'What are you waiting for? Let him have it!' whispered Silvia at Yellow-cap's elbow.

But Yellow-cap thought there was no need of hurrying; so he put the bit of paper in his pocket and said, gently pulling the King's mantle from before his face—

'My dear King, pray let us understand each other. I am sure that we can manage this thing without any trouble to either of us. As you yourself say, what need is there for me to be a usurper, if I can be a successor?'

'Ah, it's very kind of you to think of that,'

replied the King, shaking his head ; 'but I couldn't be guilty of such inhospitality as to hinder a stranger from carrying out so capital a plot. No—say no more. I see how it is. You have taken a great deal of trouble about this conspiracy, and so far you have managed it very well. I shall not interfere with your triumph for the sake of a selfish whim of my own. Never, my dear boy, never! My spirit is too royal to stoop to such meanness. And I think it unkind of you to expect such a thing of me ; and if you don't stop it I shall have to tell the executioner to cut off your head.'

'That last argument of yours is a strong one, and rather than drive you to such extremities I would let you have it your own way,' said Yellow-cap. 'But still I think this affair can be arranged. All I want, you see, is to sit on your throne ; to make a rhyme to your name, and to trample you under the feet of the metrical system. Have nothing to do with that. Come, oblige me this once, and I will do as much for you the next time.'

The King stroked his long white beard thoughtfully.

'The fact is,' he said at length, 'I am rather in a muddle about the whole business. If it had been a simple pantomime I could have seen through it; but this combination of two rival performances in one is beyond me. Let me consider. Hum! Ha! I have it. Let us draw lots from the donkey!'

'Draw lots from the donkey?' repeated Yellow-cap, puzzled in his turn.

'To be sure—the way we always do it— draw lots of hair, you know, from the donkey's tail,' continued his Majesty, brightening up, and turning back the ruffles from his wrists. 'The way it is done is this: we each of us in turn pull out a handful; and the one that makes the donkey kick first wins the match.'

'Very well,' said Yellow-cap, 'I agree, on condition that you take the first pull.'

'Such courtesy shows the true prince,' replied the King, with a pleased smile. 'I accept the favour as frankly as it was offered. Ho! fellows, back the animal round there— give him plenty of room to kick—so. Now, then, my lords and gentlemen, make a circle round us, and mark his tail with care. And do you, Mr. Chancellor of the Jingle, act as umpire.'

Everything having been thus arranged, and amidst a pause of breathless interest, his Transparent Majesty King Ormund, Emperor of Great Britain, France, and Ireland, and Defender of the Faith, advanced on tiptoe towards the donkey, who, not suspecting what was to come, stood with its hind quarters turned to him, its head being held fast by the half-witted driver.

When within about two feet of the donkey's heels the monarch stopped, and stretching out his arm, he grasped with his hand the long tuft of hair which grew at the end of the animal's tail. Then by a sudden motion he gave it such a tug as might almost have fetched the tail itself out by the roots.

Without an instant's delay the donkey kicked out as if it wanted to put its hoofs through the skylight in the roof of the theatre; but, King Ormund's stomach happening to be in the way, that potentate was lifted from the ground and made to pass through the air in a graceful curve. He came down upon the upturned face of the Chancellor of the Jingle (who was too busy with his duties as umpire to notice his danger) and flattened him out upon the stage in such a way as to make it quite impossible for him to give his decision.

CHAPTER X.

UPON this tableau the curtain came down ;
but the applause was really so deafening that
all the performers—including, of course, the
King and the donkey—had to come out and
pass before the footlights : when the donkey
got a bouquet, and the King a bunch of
turniptops. They then returned to the stage
and took their places as before, and the curtain went up again.

During several seconds the King lay quite
still, with the Chancellor underneath him ;
and Yellow-cap began to feel uneasy, for he
reflected that if the King should lie still per-
manently his own position might become
awkward. He spoke of this in a low tone
to Silvia, who was coquetting with her sweetheart the donkey-driver across the donkey's
back.

'No need to be alarmed, your Lordship,'

replied she composedly. 'His Majesty is only a little out of breath. The stomach of an hereditary monarch is, you know, the strongest thing about him. He will be all right directly.'

In fact, hardly had she done speaking when the King gave a cough and raised himself to a sitting posture. He really seemed none the worse for what had happened; in spite of which Yellow-cap could not help feeling glad that he had not been in the King's place.

'Where is the Chancellor of the Jingle?' demanded the King as soon as he could speak. 'Why does he not come forward and give his judgment as umpire? Where is he, I say? By my crown and sceptre if he does not appear and answer this instant I will have his head cut off!'

'Pardon me, my dear sir,' said Yellow-cap, 'if I say that the Chancellor would probably have given his judgment before now, if you had not yourself put difficulties in the way of his doing so. You are _t this moment sitting upon the man's face, and it would therefore be impossible if not disrespectful for him to say anything until your Majesty has

arisen.   If you will let me pull you up he
will be ready to obey your commands—unless,' he added aside to Silvia, ' he is actually
crushed to death.'

'No fear of that,' Silvia replied cheerfully.   ' The face of a real Chancellor of the
Jingle is the most impenetrable thing about
him ; and I have no doubt that he is smiling
at this very minute.'

And in fact hardly had the King raised
himself erect than the Chancellor jumped to
his feet, with a most charming smile; and
having bowed to the King, to Yellow-cap,
and to the audience, he spoke thus :—

'In the drawing of lots his Transparent
Majesty King Ormund has been successful ;
and therefore his Royal Highness Prince
Yellow-cap has won the wager.'

'Capital—capital!' exclaimed the King,
rubbing his hands and stamping about the
stage gleefully.   ' But you,' he added, turning
to the Chancellor of the Jingle, ' must, of
course, have your head cut off just the same.'

At this a couple of halberdiers approached
and laid their hands on the culprit's shoulders.

Yellow-cap had at first thought that to
lose his head would serve the Chancellor only

right; but, as he was averse to bloodshed, and as his own affairs seemed to be going on so prosperously, he resolved to be merciful.

'Allow me a word,' he said. 'Since I have won the wager I thereby succeed to King Ormund's throne and sceptre, and by virtue of the power in me vested I do hereby extend to the Chancellor my royal clemency. Loose him, halberdiers, on your allegiance!'

The halberdiers hesitated; and King Ormund, stroking his beard meditatively, said, 'I'm not sure about this. You haven't been crowned yet, you know.'

'At all events I am as much king as anybody here,' Yellow-cap replied firmly. 'And meanwhile I advise anybody who cares to keep his head on his shoulders to obey my commands.'

'I'll tell you what we might do,' exclaimed the King brightly: 'we might draw lots——'

'No; I refuse to leave affairs of State to chance. But, in order to oblige you in every way I can, I will appoint the Chancellor of the Jingle referee. He shall decide whether or not his head is to be cut off; and I promise to abide by his decision.'

'Hum!' said the King. 'Ha! well, that certainly does seem fair. Besides, one must have some consideration for the poor donkey. I agree, then. Now, Mr. Chancellor, what is your decision?'

'My head stays where it is, please your Majesty,' replied the Chancellor promptly.

'It's astonishing what a run of luck you are having!' exclaimed the King, turning to Yellow-cap, with a sigh of admiration. 'Pray, are you as fortunate in love as you seem to be in everything else?'

At this question there rose in Yellow-cap's mind the picture of a little square room, with bright walls and clean sanded floor; a churn in one corner, and a brightly polished tin pan upon the dresser in place of a looking-glass. In this room stood a lovely young girl, with tears in her eyes, but a smile dimpling her rosy cheeks. She was looking up with a loving glance at a young man, who was fastening round her neck, by a bit of ribbon, the half of a spade guinea. Yellow-cap passed his hand over his eyes: the picture had vanished.

'What are you dreaming about?' said the voice of Silvia in his ear. 'The half of a brass farthing is just as good, if you will only think so. And you have not yet answered his Majesty's question.'

'Ah! I beg pardon,' muttered Yellow-cap. 'I—what did you say? I—yes—that is—no! No, I am not so fortunate in love as I seem to be in other things. Ah me! Rosamund!'

'Well, well,' said the King, with a particularly arch look, 'I dare say we shall be able to do you a good turn in that way too.'

'Is this the place where kings are crowned?' demanded Yellow-cap.

'Certainly; where else could it be?' returned the King.

'Then I will be crowned this moment,' said Yellow-cap in the commanding tone which he had found it best to use towards these London people. 'Is there an Arch-bishop present? And let somebody fetch a throne!'

'Here is the throne, please your Worship,' said the half-witted youth, leading forward the donkey.

'And here is the Archbishop, at your service,' said one of the persons in the white dominoes, making a bow.

'That won't do,' said Yellow-cap
sharply. 'You are the Prime Maniac—only
you have shaved your moustachios.'

'That makes all the difference, please
your Highness,' replied the other humbly.

'And now I look at you again,' continued
Yellow-cap, 'I think I remember you before
you were a Prime Maniac. I remember you
when you were only three feet high.'

'It is all the same,' answered the other
again. 'I rise to the occasion.'

'Well, it makes no difference, I suppose,'
said Yellow-cap, after a pause, bestriding the
donkey's back. 'Now for the crown!'

King Ormund took the crown from his
brow and handed it to the Archbishop, who
put it on Yellow-cap's head, over the yellow
cap. Then all the courtiers round about murmured their congratulations, the audience that
filled the theatre shouted 'Hooray!' and 'En-
core!' the ex-King clapped him on the shoulder and said, 'Bless you, my boy!' and Silvia
whispered in his ear, 'Now you are King!'

'Long live King Yellow-cap!' roared
everybody.

'How do you like it?' asked Ormund
pleasantly.

' I feel about as I did before,' replied the
new King, in a slightly disappointed tone.
' How much does this crown weigh ?   Haven't
you a lighter one ? '

' No ; and you won't find that one grow
any lighter,' said Ormund, with a chuckle.
' But if you don't feel any difference I do !   I
am ten years younger already.   I am posi
tively light-headed.'

' Well, at all events I am a King ! ' said
Yellow-cap.

' And now,' observed Ormund, rubbing
his hands and glancing at Silvia, ' since the
coronation is over, what do you say to our
having the wedding ? '

' Yes—yes ; the wedding ! ' echoed all the
courtiers.

Silvia arranged the ribbon at her throat,
looked coquettishly at King Yellow-cap, and
murmured in his ear—

' What says your Majesty ?   There is no
time like the present.'

' Wedding ! ' repeated King Yellow-cap,
turning from one to another.   ' Whose wedding ? '

' Whose but your own, gracious liege ! '
replied the courtiers.

'My own! Nonsense! Whom should I marry?'

'Whom but Silvia, most puissant prince?' said the courtiers again.

'Silvia? Why, she is barmaid at the inn! And besides, she is engaged to marry somebody else.'

'Ah, you mean the Prince of Sprats,' remarked the ex-King. 'But that match is broken off. Since you are on the throne he is in opposition, and can only be considered a pretender; but Silvia is a princess of the blood, cousin-german of the dynasty, and Columbine into the bargain; so she can marry nobody but you.'

'That fellow who owns the donkey the Prince of Sprats?' cried Yellow-cap. 'He the son of King Ormund?'

'Prince Assimund—yes. I spoke to you of him yesterday. A little queer in the head, you know, but that is only a sign of his royalty.'

'All this may be so,' replied Yellow-cap, stroking his chin; 'but as to my marrying Silvia—that seems rather sudden.'

'Not more sudden than agreeable, if I were in your place,' observed the ex-King, with a twinkle in his eye which made the pit laugh.

'Besides,' continued Yellow-cap, 'I have an indistinct notion that once—somewhere— I loved—but, no! What with the cap and crown together I can remember nothing. And perhaps Silvia may be she, after all ; she looks something like her ; but yet——'

'If your Majesty will let me hang this half of a brass farthing round your neck,' interrupted Silvia, 'you will have no more doubts about the matter.' And as she spoke she held the farthing towards him, with a mischievous smile.

'But don't you care at all for Assimund?' he asked her.

'The interests of the State are supreme,' returned, Silvia with a grand air.

'Well, if I must, I must,' said King Yellow-cap rather ungraciously. 'But I thought the Kings of England could do what they pleased.'

'Oh, dear, no,' exclaimed the Archbishop, 'Magna Charta forbid !'

'Then I wish——' began Yellow-cap.

But he paused. What had he left to wish ?

He stretched out his hand to take the half of the brass farthing.

At that moment there was a great noise and confusion at the back of the stage, and half the audience sprang to their feet, supposing that the theatre had caught fire. But out of the confusion was dragged forward a sort of cart, in which a number of persons were seated, with veils over their faces, and their hands tied behind their backs. Yellow-cap saw that one of these persons was a woman.

CHAPTER XI.

THE GRAND TRANSFORMATION SCENE.

'WHAT is that? What people are those in the cart?' demanded Yellow-cap, rising in his stirrups to get a better view.

'Please your Majesty they are prisoners of State,' said the Home Doggerel, who had turned rather pale. 'It is quite a mistake their coming here; they should have been taken to another theatre. However, since they are here your Majesty cannot do better than sign their death-warrant. I have a pen and ink here; or, if your Majesty happens not to know how to sign your name, I can——'

'Hold your tongue,' interrupted Yellow-cap sharply. He was looking very hard at the veiled figure of the woman. After a pause he said—

'Before signing my name (which I am perfectly able to do) to the death-warrant I will know what crime these persons have

I

committed.   Tell them to come nearer, that
I may question them.'

'Sire,' exclaimed the Home Doggerel, in
evident dismay, 'the law of England does
not permit an accused person to be ques-
tioned.'

'Why not?'

'Because it might lead to a discovery.'

'What discovery?'

'The discovery of the truth, Sire; and
where would you and all of us be then?'

At this a man in the pit began to hiss,
and the police tried to take him into custody;
but they could not find out his address, and
therefore let him alone.

'Where would we be indeed!' murmured
King Yellow-cap thoughtfully.   'Nevertheless,' he continued, again fixing his eyes upon
the veiled woman, 'I am resolved to question
these people; and this pantomime shall not
go on until I have done so.'

'I humbly beg your Majesty to think
what you are about,' said the Lord Privy
Gander in an agitated tone; 'you are in
danger not only of hearing the truth but of
violating etiquette.'

'It might bring about a reform,' added

the First Lord of the Seesaw, with a shudder.

'At all events let the woman be condemned unheard,' said Silvia. 'She looks dangerous, and may intend to do your Majesty some harm.'

'Be silent, everyone!' thundered King Yellow-cap at the top of his voice. 'I say I will hear these persons, and I will hear the woman first. Stop—where is the Headsman?'

'Here I be, your Majesty, quite at your service,' said the Headsman, shouldering through the crowd, and saluting the young King with his axe. He was an immensely strong man, seven feet high, with short red hair standing up over his head, and a butcher's apron tied on in front of him.

'Headsman,' said the King, 'if anyone stirs or says a word except by my leave, off with his head! Do you understand?'

For answer the Headsman tossed his terrible axe high up in the air, caught it lightly as it came down, and then, swinging it round his head, he cut off the tall feather that was fastened in the cap of the Chancellor

of the Jingle. An inch more would have
buried the blade in his skull.

'Very good,' said King Yellow-cap; 'I
see you know your business. Now, then,.
bring me hither that cart. Let the woman
come down.'

Amidst a total silence, during which the
Headsman was seen to feel the edge of his.
axe with his thumb—keeping his right eye
upon King Yellow-cap the while, and the
left upon the Home Doggerel—the veiled
woman got down from the cart and came
forward to the donkey which served the
King as a throne. Here she dropped a.
curtsey.

King Yellow-cap gazed steadfastly upon
her for several moments. The black veil
still hung before her face, but round her neck
was visible a bit of pink ribbon.

'Who are you?' he asked at last.

'I am a village maiden, Sire,' she answered in a voice so sweet and clear that it
was heard all over the theatre.

'Of what crime are you accused?'

'Of high treason, Sire.'

'In what way did you commit it?'

At this question the Home Doggerel

and the other members of the Cabinet made
a movement as if they wished to step behind
the scenes ; but King Yellow-cap noticed it,
and in an awful voice he cried out—

' Headsman ! '

' Ready, your Majesty,' said that officer,
poising his axe to strike.

' One step more,' said the King, turning
to the six courtiers, ' and your heads fly into
the pit. Keep your axe poised,' he added
to the Headsman.

' Right you are, young man ! ' said the
person in the pit whom the police had tried
to arrest for hissing. ' Right you are, Master
Yellow-cap ; you're just about the sort of
king I goes in for, and so I tells you.'

' And now go on with your story,' said
the King to the veiled woman.

' May it please your Majesty,' she replied,
" the way it happened was this. As I was
taking the butter out of my churn yesterday
afternoon there came into my dairy-room an
ugly little long-armed man, with a hook nose
and a great pair of moustachios. I asked
him what he wanted, and he said that he
wanted me, and that I had promised to
marry him.'

'Ha!' said King Yellow-cap. 'And what did you say to that?'

'I was very indignant, Sire,' said the maiden, 'because I had that very day promised to wed a young man of our own village, whom I had known and loved for many years. But this ugly dwarf said, "You belong to me; and to prove it, here is the other half of the spade guinea that is hanging round your neck!" Now, Sire, when I parted with the young man whom I love he had cut his spade guinea in two, and each of us had kept half, for a sign by which, as he said, we might know each other when we met, no matter what changes had come over us in the meantime. So, when I saw the token in this dwarf's hand, I feared my lover was dead, because I knew that no enchantment could make him look like the dwarf, and I could not believe that he would have given up his half of our spade guinea while he had life enough left to guard it.'

'Might your lover not have given it up for something that seemed to him more precious?' asked the young King in a tremulous voice.

'No,' said the maiden firmly, 'for he loved me, and nothing in this world is so precious as love.'

'Go on with your story,' said the King.

'There is little more to tell, please your Majesty. I told the dwarf to be gone; but he threw his arms round me and tried to carry me away. Then I screamed out, and all the young men in the village ran up, and there was a great fight. Then the dwarf said that he was the Lord High Sheepstealer of England, and that he arrested us all for high treason. So he bound us and tied veils over our faces, and brought us prisoners to London; and this morning we were carried hither in this cart.'

'And what do you wish me to do for you?' asked the King.

'I do not much care what becomes of me, Sire,' replied the maiden, 'for I fear my lover is dead, and if he is, then all the love I had for the world is dead with him. But if your Majesty would find out whether he still lives and loves me I will thank you more than for my life, and I will be content to die.'

'You shall have your wish,' said the King, 'though I fear your lover is not worthy of you. But first your eyes shall be unveiled, and you shall tell me whether, amidst this assembly, you can find the man who called himself the Lord High Sheepstealer of England.'

And now a wonderful thing happened.

When the six courtiers, in their white dominoes, heard the command of the King that the maiden's eyes should be unveiled they all got behind one another, and cowered down, shaking in their shoes. And when the maiden's glance rested on them they cowered down still more, as if they were trying to hide their heads in their necks and their necks in their shoulders. Still they shrivelled and shrunk, until they no longer appeared like six tall courtiers, but like half a dozen ugly little dwarfs, barely three feet high. And when they saw how small they had become they uttered a cry of terror, and seemed to rush into one another's arms. And with that —though how it came about would be impossible to say—there stood only a single dwarf, a great deal stouter and uglier than the six, but with precisely the same cast of features and general appearance.

' That is the creature that called itself the

Lord High Sheepstealer of England,' said the maiden.

'What have you to say for yourself, sirrah?' said the King sternly.

'Mercy! spare my life!' cried the dwarf, falling on his knees. 'And bethink yourself that we are brothers, and that in destroying me you would unmake yourself.'

'That is the very thing that decides me to show you no mercy,' answered King Yellow-cap. 'I am sick of all this stage-play.'

'Have a care what you do, Sire,' said Silvia, with a frown on her face, which looked much older and less pretty than it had done hitherto. 'He is your brother, and you are bound to him by the vows of the Order.'

'I shall know how to break those bonds,' Yellow-cap replied. 'In the first place, let my guards loose all the prisoners who are in the cart and let them go free.'

When this had been done he turned to the village maiden.

'Get up behind me on the donkey,' he said, 'and put your arms round my waist.'

The maiden obeyed, the donkey standing quite still, and not so much as moving the end of its tail.

'Now let Assimund, Prince of Sprats, approach,' said the King.

'People of England,' he then continued, facing the audience, 'I have been King over you for half an hour, and I have had enough of it. But, before abdicating, I will place the crown on brows worthier to wear it than mine. Behold Prince Assimund, no longer a pretender, but to be hereafter your absolute and legitimate monarch. And behold Silvia, his fitting queen and consort, whose hand I place in his.' He suited the action to the word, and then, removing the crown, he set it upon Assimund's head.

But the audience murmured, and seemed dissatisfied; and Silvia smiled maliciously; and even the dwarf, over whom the Headsman was standing with uplifted axe, showed his teeth in an ugly grin.

'Silence!' shouted Yellow-cap. 'I have not yet done. Headsman—strike!'

Down came the heavy axe; and everyone thought that the dwarf must be cloven asunder from head to foot. But before the axe could reach him there was no dwarf there. Whether he melted into nothing, or whether he disappeared down one of those trap-doors which are to be found in every stage, or what else became of him, will probably never be known. At all events the blade of the axe came down upon the bare boards and buried itself six inches deep in the wood, and no dwarf was there, but only the glittering half of a spade guinea, strung on a broken thread of silk. This the Headsman placed in Yellow-cap's hand, and he hid it in his bosom.

'He lives still!' said Silvia, smiling again.

'But he will never again cross my path,' replied Yellow-cap. 'King Assimund,' he added, 'accept my parting gift before I go. With this and with your crown, and with Silvia to whisper worldly wisdom in your ear, it will be your own fault if you are not the mightiest sovereign in Christendom.'

So saying he snatched off the yellow cap from his own black locks and clapped it down upon Assimund's foolish poll. At the same moment he felt the arms of the village maiden tighten round his waist.

He struck his heels into the donkey's sides and shook the rein. The donkey kicked up its heels, and seemed to spring bodily off the stage. Yellow-cap (but he was now Yellow-cap no longer) had a momentary glimpse of Assimund, now wearing an aspect of imperial magnificence, of Silvia, frowning and biting her lip, and of the whole great audience standing up and shouting; and then he had a feeling of passing rapidly through the air he knew not whither. . . . . .

He came down very softly.

It was high noon. They were in the meadow beside the river. The donkey was feeding quietly near at hand; Raymond had fallen on his knees in the grass, and Rosamund was standing before him.

'Oh, Rosamund,' he said. 'you are my kingdom! Will you take me back?'

'You have been a very naughty boy,' she replied, 'and you deserve a scolding. But come home first and have some milk, for you must be hungry.'

Raymond looked up at her. She was more lovely than ever. There was a sparkle of laughter in her eyes and a beautiful blush in her cheeks. Beyond her rose the thatched roofs of Honeymead, overshadowed by the great lime-trees; the birds were singing, and the sky was blue.

'Come—do get up!' exclaimed Rosamund. 'Now that you belong to me you

must give up these mooning dreamy ways of
yours and behave sensibly. Come—make
haste! Armand, and Dorimund, and all the
rest of them have been invited, and our
betrothal is to be formally announced.'

, 'How strange all this sounds!' said Raymond, getting to his feet in a bewildered
way. 'You almost make me think that I have
been——'

Before he could finish his sentence the
donkey lifted its head and tail in the air and
sent forth a long-drawn reproachful bray.

'Ah! no, it was real—I have not been
dreaming,' Raymond said. 'If it had not
been for that donkey where should we be
now?'

'How stupid you are to-day—muttering
to yourself like that!' cried Rosamund,
briskly. 'Anyone would think you had a
headache.'

'And so I had—a very bad one,' said
Raymond.

Rosamund became tender immediately.

'Oh, my poor love!' murmured she.
'And what a horrid red mark that is round
your forehead, as if you had been wearing a
cap that was too tight for you. Stoop down

a little—let me kiss it.   There, does that feel
better ? '

'A great deal better,' Raymond answered, with a long sigh.

So they went back, hand in hand, through
the meadow.   The breeze came fresh and
sweet upon their faces ; they smelt the fragrance of the breath of cows.   As they approached their home they walked more and
more slowly.   Rosamund was humming a
little song to herself ; she was as happy as a
bird.

But Raymond was silent, and pondered
many things.

RUMPTY-DUDGET

CHAPTER I.

THE PALACE AND THE TOWER.

IN the days before the sun caught fire, before
the moon froze up, and before you were born,
a great queen had three children, whose
names were Hilda, Harold, and Hector.
Princess Hilda, who was the eldest, had blue
eyes and golden hair; Prince Hector, who
was the youngest, had black eyes and black
hair; and Prince Harold, who was neither
the youngest nor the eldest, had, of course,
brown eyes and brown hair. There was
nothing else specially remarkable about them,
except that they were (at the time I write of)
the best children in the world, as well as the
prettiest and the cleverest for their age; that
they lived in the most beautiful palace ever
built, and that the garden they played in was
the loveliest ever seen.

The palace stood on the borders of a
mighty forest, on the further side of which

K

lay Fairyland. But there was only one window in the palace that looked out upon this forest, and that was the round window of the room in which Hilda, Harold, and Hector slept. And since the round window was never open except at night, after the three children had been put to bed, they knew very little about how the forest looked, or what kind of flowers grew there, or what sort of birds sang in the dark branches of the lofty trees. Sometimes, however, as they lay with their three heads on their three pillows, and with all their eyes open, waiting for the Spirit of Forgetfulness to come and fasten down their eyelids, they would see stars, white, blue, and red, twinkling in the sky overhead ; and below, amongst the gloomy shadows of the trees, other yellow stars which danced about and flitted to and fro. These flitting stars were supposed by grown-up people to be will-o'-the-wisp, jack-o'-lanterns, fire-flies, and glow-worms. But the three children knew them to be the torches borne by the elves as they capered hither and thither about their affairs. For although the Forest of Mystery (as it was named) was not, strictly speaking, in Fairyland, but formed the boundary between that and the rest of the world, yet many fairies held nightly revels there. The children wished that a few of these tiny people would come in through the round window some evening and pay them a visit. But if such a thing ever happened it was not until after the children had fallen asleep; and then, when they woke up in the morning, they had forgotten all about it.

The garden was on the side of the palace opposite to the Forest of Mystery; it was called the Garden of Delight. It was full of flowers, pink, white, and blue; and there were birds, and fountains, in the marble basins of which gold-fishes glowed and swam. In the centre of the garden was a round green lawn for the children to play on; but at the end of the garden was a tall thick hedge, on which no blossoms ever grew, and which was prickly with sharp-pointed leaves and thorns. This hedge also had a name, but the children did not know what it was. It was impossible either to get round the hedge, or to get over it, or to get through it—except in one place, where a small opening had been made. But through that opening no one might pass, for the land on the other side belonged to a dwarf, whose name was Rumpty-Dudget, and whose only pleasure lay in doing mischief. An ugly little dwarf he was, all grey from head to foot. He wore a broad-brimmed grey hat, a thick grey beard, and a grey cloak that was so much too long for him that it trailed on the ground like a grey tail as he walked. On his back was a grey hump, which made him look even shorter than he was—and he was not much over a foot high at his tallest. He lived in a large grey tower, whose battlements the three children could see rising above the hedge as they played on the round lawn; and over the tower there hung, even in the brightest weather, a dull grey cloud.

Inside the tower was a vast room with a hundred and one corners to it : and in each of the corners stood a little child, with its face to the wall and its hands behind its back. Who were the children, and how came they there ? They were children, whom Rumpty-Dudget had caught trespassing on his grounds, and had therefore carried away with him to his tower. In this way he had filled up one corner after another, until only one corner was left unfilled ; and that one, curiously enough,

was the one-hundred-and-first. Now, it was
a well-known fact that if Rumpty-Dudget
could but catch a child to put it in that one
empty corner he would become master of all
the country round about. And since he loved
nothing that was not of the same colour and
temper as himself, the noble palace would in
that case disappear, the garden would be
changed into a desert covered with grey
stones and brambles, and the dull grey cloud
that now hung above the tower would sullenly spread itself over all the heavens. The
mighty Forest of Mystery, too, would be cut
down and sold for firewood; and the elves
and fairies would fly westward in pursuit of
the flying sun. You may be sure, therefore,
that Rumpty-Dudget tried with all his might
to get hold of a child to put into that hundred-
and-first corner. But by this time the in-
habitants of the country had begun to realise
their danger; and all the mothers were so
careful, and all the children were so obedient,
that, for a long time, the hundred-and-first
corner remained empty.

CHAPTER II.

THE AUNT, THE CAT, AND THE DWARF.

WHEN Hilda, Harold, and Hector were still very young indeed the Queen, their mother, was obliged to make a long journey to a far-off country, and to leave her children behind her. But before going she took them in her arms and said, 'My darlings, though I must leave you, you will not be left alone, either by night or by day. While you are awake you will be protected by a beautiful white cat that I shall send to you, named Tom; and while you are asleep your fairy aunt will keep watch over you; you will not see her, but you will know that she is with you by your pleasant dreams. Only at one hour of the day will you be left unguarded, and that is the hour before sunset. At that hour Tom will have to be away, and your fairy aunt will not yet have arrived, so you must be very careful of yourselves. You will, I hope, try always

to be good children ; but in the hour before
sunset you must try twenty-four times harder
than ever. Nobody knows what may happen
when a little child does wrong ; but there is
great danger that the sun might catch fire
and the moon freeze up. So, once more, my
darlings, be very careful ; for every hour is
as long as it is short, but the hour before sunset is the longest and the shortest of all.'

The children promised to remember ; and
their mother kissed them and went away.
The same day Tom the Cat arrived. A
beautiful big cat he was, with deep soft fur,
round yellow eyes, and a tail as thick as a
feather duster. He was also the sweetest-
tempered cat in the world, so that the children
lived with him several years without even so
much as suspecting that he had such a thing
as a claw about him. He could purr as comfortably as the hopper of a windmill ; and he
took care of the children better than a dozen
nurses would have done. But an hour before
sunset every day he always·disappeared, and
only came back again when the last bit of the
sun had gone out of sight. Then he put the
children to bed, and purred outside their
window until they fell asleep ; and as soon as

that happened in floated the Fairy Aunt, to kiss their closed eyelids, and to hover beside their beds and whisper in their ears all manner of charming stories about Fairyland, and the wonderful things that were to be seen and done there. But early in the morning, just before they awoke, she would kiss their eyelids once more and flit away out of the round window; and the white cat, with his yellow eyes and his thick tail, would come purring comfortably in at the door.

One day, however (the unluckiest day in the whole year), Hilda, Harold, and Hector went out to play as usual on the round lawn in the centre of the garden. It was Rumpty-Dudget's birthday—the only day in the whole year on which he had power to creep through the hole in the hedge and prowl about the Queen's grounds. Nevertheless, all went well until the last hour before sunset, when Tom the Cat was forced to be away. Before he went he warned the children to look out for the grey rat; but before he had time to explain what he meant by the grey rat the hour struck, and he could not help vanishing. The children were left to themselves; but they were not at all frightened. They had

never heard of Rumpty-Dudget; and this is
not so strange as it might at first seem; for it
often happens in the world that our worst
enemies live so close to us that we are not
aware of them until after we have fallen into
their power. Hilda, Harold, and Hector, at
all events, went on playing together very
kindly; for up to this time they had never
had a quarrel. The only thing that troubled
them was, that Tom the Cat was not there to
play with them; they all longed to see his
yellow eyes and his thick tail, and to stroke
his soft back, and hear his comfortable purr.
But it was now very near sunset, and he must
soon return. The sun, like a great red ball,
hung a little way above the edge of the world;
though he had not caught fire as yet, he was
evidently very hot, and it was quite time for
him to be at rest.

All at once Princess Hilda, who had been
gazing at the sun with her blue eyes wide
open, heard a little croaking laugh, and looking down, she saw a strange little creature
standing close beside her, all grey from head
to foot. He wore a grey hat and beard, and
a long grey cloak that dragged on the ground
like a tail, and on his back was a grey hump

that made him seem even shorter than he was,
though at the most he was hardly over a foot
high. Hilda was surprised, but not in the
least frightened, for nobody had ever yet done
her any harm; and besides, this odd little
grey man, though he was as ugly as a rent in
a new pinafore, grinned at her from one ear
to the other, and seemed to be the most good-
natured dwarf in the world. So Princess
Hilda called to Prince Harold and Prince
Hector, who, when they saw what had come
to them, were no more frightened than Hilda,
and a good deal more amused ; and as the
dwarf kept on grinning from one ear to the
other the three children began to smile back
at him. Meanwhile the great red ball of the
sun was slowly dropping downwards; and
now his lower rim was just resting on the
edge of the world.

Since you have already heard about
Rumpty-Dudget you will have guessed that
this grey dwarf was none other than he, and
that although he grinned so broadly from one
ear to the other he wished in reality to do the
three children harm ; and even (if he could
manage it) to carry one of them off to his
tower, to stand in the hundred-and-first

corner, with his face to the wall and his hands behind his back. But Rumpty-Dudget had no power to do this so long as the children stayed on their side of the prickly hedge; he must first tempt them to creep through the opening, and then, when they were upon his own grounds, he could do with them what he pleased. Now, the children had often been warned not to creep through the hedge, both by their Queen-mother, before she went away, and by their Fairy Aunt in dreams, and by Tom the Cat in the day-time; and as they had never had reason to suppose that there was anything prettier on the other side of the hedge than on their own, they had never thought of going thither. Rumpty-Dudget knew this; and as he was even more cunning than he was ugly he had made up his mind to profit by it.

'My dear young people,' he said, holding out his hands, 'I am very glad to meet you. It has grieved me to see you all playing here on this ugly lawn, when there is a garden so much more beautiful just on the other side of the hedge. I am very fond of children, and I make it my business to amuse them. If you will just give yourselves the trouble to

step through that opening in the hedge you
shall see something that you never saw
before.'

The three children thought this sounded
very pleasant; but, after a pause, Princess
Hilda, who generally took the lead, said :

'We were told not to go on the other
side of the hedge.'

'Who could have been so unkind as to
tell you that ?' cried Rumpty-Dudget, as if
he was very much shocked. 'Besides, one
side of the hedge is just the same as another;
and if it is wrong to go on the other side,
how much more wrong it must be to stay on
this !'

Hilda thought awhile before answering,
for what Rumpty-Dudget had said certainly
sounded reasonable. 'But why,' she asked
at last, 'should there be any hedge at all ?'

'It is all on account of the hole through
it,' the dwarf replied, with his most charming
grin. 'There could have been no hole, you
see, if there hadn't been a hedge; and that is
why the hedge was planted.'

Princess Hilda could not deny that this
was true ; and, moreover, since she had
begun to talk with the dwarf she had felt a

strong desire to see whether the garden on
the other side of the hedge was so very much
prettier than their own, as he declared.
'What do you say, boys?' she asked, turning
to the two little princes. 'Shall we take just
one peep?'

'That is right! Come, my dears, at
once!' put in Rumpty-Dudget eagerly, taking
Hilda and Harold each by the hand, and
letting little Hector trot on before. 'It is
already late, and I want you to see my
garden before the sun goes down.' So they
all came to the opening in the hedge; and, if
the truth must be told, the three children
were almost as anxious to get through it as
Rumpty-Dudget was to have them do so.
And the great red ball of the sun kept going
down further and further, and now all his
lower half was out of sight beneath the edge
of the world.

'Now, my dear,' said Rumpty-Dudget to
Princess Hilda, 'will you step through first?
Ladies always go first, you know.'

'Not through holes in the hedges,' replied Hilda, drawing back. 'It is always
the men who go first then.'

All but the last quarter of the sun was

now hidden behind the edge of the world, and there was no time to be lost, for (as Rumpty-Dudget well knew) as soon as the sun was quite gone Tom the Cat would appear. So he said, as amiably as he could, though in reality he felt very angry :

'Well, then, Prince Harold, my fine fellow, you are the next eldest; take my hand, and in we go.'

'No,' said Prince Harold, drawing back; 'I think I am too big to get through that little hole. Somebody else must go first.'

Rumpty-Dudget trembled with rage and fear; and there was only the smallest bit of the sun yet visible. However, he managed to say, in a tolerably smooth voice :

'Little Prince Hector, there, is my man after all! He will come through the hole, and see the pretty things, won't he ?'

Now, Prince Hector· was a sturdy little fellow, and afraid of nothing; so he put his hand in Rumpty-Dudget's and said boldly :

'Yes, I'll go; but if your garden isn't any prettier than you are I shan't want to stay long.'

'Let me lift you in, my little hero,' said Rumpty-Dudget, taking Hector round the

waist with his little bony hands; 'and I'll
warrant you won't come back in a hurry.
Now, then—jump!'

But just at that moment the last scrap
of the sun vanished beneath the edge of the
world; and instantly, with a tremendous
hissing and caterwauling, Tom the Cat came
springing across the lawn like a white-hot
snowball. His yellow eyes flashed, his back
bristled, and every hair upon his tail stood
out so straight that the tail looked as thick
as an old-fashioned muff. He flew straight
at Rumpty-Dudget and leaped upon his
hump, and bit and scratched him soundly.
Rumpty-Dudget yelled with pain, and dropping Prince Hector, he vanished through the
hole in the hedge like a hot chestnut into a
hungry boy.

But from the other side of the hedge he
flung at the three children a handful of
black mud; a bit of it hit Princess Hilda on
the forehead, and another bit fell upon Prince
Harold's nose, and another upon little Prince
Hector's chin. And there those three black
spots stayed; and all the washing and scrub-
bing in the world would not make them go
away. It is always so with the mud that

Rumpty-Dudget throws; it seems to grow down into you until it fastens a root in your heart. And this, probably, was the reason why Princess Hilda (who had until then been the best little girl in the world) began from that time to wish to rule things; and Prince Harold (who had until then been one of the two best little boys in the world) began from that time to wish to have things; and little Prince Hector (who had until then been the other of the two best little boys in the world, began from that time to wish to do things which he was told not to do.

Such was the effect of Rumpty-Dudget's three mud-spots.

CHAPTER III.

THE WAYS OF THE WIND.

But, although Hilda, Harold, and Hector were no longer quite the best children in the world, they were pretty good children as the world goes, and if it had not been for the north wind they would have got on together very well. But whenever that wind blew everything began to go wrong. Hilda wanted everything her own way; Harold wanted everything in his own pockets; and Hector wanted everything at cross-purposes. Then, too, the spots on Hilda's forehead, on Harold's nose, and on Hector's chin became blacker and blacker, and hotter and hotter, until the children were ready to cry from pain and vexation. But tears could do no more than soap and water to wash the spots away.

As soon as the wind began to blow from the south, however, the spots began to lose

L

their blackness, and the pricking to lessen, until at last the children almost forgot their trouble. Yet it never altogether disappeared; and neither Tom the Cat nor the Fairy Aunt had the power to cure it. But Tom used to say that, unless Hilda and her two brothers would agree always to make the wind blow from the south, the hundred-and-first corner in Rumpty-Dudget's tower would sooner or later be filled.

'How can we make the wind blow one way or the other?' Hilda would ask.

'It all depends upon you, nevertheless,' Tom would reply. 'Winds do not move of themselves, but people pull them.'

'Well, I don't understand it,' Hilda would answer, after a little thinking; 'and if I don't, of course the boys don't either.'

At night, when the Fairy Aunt came in through the round window, and sat on their bedside to whisper stories about Fairyland into their ears, the children would sometimes ask her to take them all three up in her arms and carry them over the tops of the trees of the Forest of Mystery to her home far away on the other side. Then she would shake her head and say:

'While those spots are on your faces you cannot come with me.'

'Why not?' the children asked in their dream.

'Because they are a sign that a part of each of you belongs to Rumpty-Dudget; and he will not let go of that part, in spite of all that I can do.'

'Shall we never be able to go with you, then?' dreamed the children piteously.

'Not until the wind blows from the south every day in the week. When that happens the spots will vanish, and I will take you all three in my arms, and fly with you over the tops of the trees to Fairyland.'

'And what shall we see there?' the children asked.

'You will see the Queen, your mother.'

'And shall we see you too?'

'Yes, I shall be with you.'

'And Tom the Cat too?'

'What you have loved in Tom the Cat will be there too,' answered the fairy, smiling.

'But how shall we make the wind blow from the south every day in the week?'

At that the fairy smiled and shook her head, and touched each one of them on the heart; and no other answer would she give. So the children were no wiser on that point than before.

Thus time went on steadily, to-morrow always going before to-day, and yesterday invariably bringing up the rear, until a year was past; and what should come round again but Rumpty-Dudget's birthday, the most unlucky day of all the three hundred and sixty five! An hour and twenty seconds before sunset Tom the Cat said to the children:

'Now, you must be very careful, while I am away, to do as I tell you. Do not go out into the garden, do not touch the black ball that lies on the nursery table, and do not jump against the north wind; for if you do——'

But at this moment the hour struck, and Tom the Cat sprang into the air and disappeared like a soap bubble.

For a while the three children remembered what had been said to them; they played quietly in the palace, and did not touch the black ball on the nursery table. But towards sunset it so happened that they were all leaning against the table, with their elbows resting on it, and their heads between

their hands. There lay the black ball mysterious and quiet. The longer the children
looked at it the more mysterious it appeared.
At last Hilda said :

'I wonder where it came from ?'

'I wonder what it's made of?' said
Harold.

'I wonder why we mustn't touch it ?' said
Hector.

Then all three looked at it steadily for
another minute. Then Hilda exclaimed suddenly :

'I believe it moved !'

'So do I !' cried Harold.

'I don't!' said Hector. 'But I can make
it move.' And with that he gave the table a
tip, and the black ball rolled off, bounced on
to the floor, and jumped out of the window
into the garden.

'You have disobeyed Tom the Cat,' said
Hilda, after a pause.

'How shall we ever get it back again ?'
cried Harold, running to the window and
looking out. 'Oh, I can see it ! there, in the
middle of the lawn.'

'Yes, but we are not to go into the
garden,' said Hilda.

'It is all Hector's fault,' said Harold.

'I am going into the garden to play with the ball,' said Hector boldly; and he walked off.

'What a naughty boy he is!' said Harold to Hilda.

'Yes; but the wind blows from the south,' she answered. 'You may stay here if you like; I think I shall go and play with Hector.' And she walked off.

'What naughty children they are!' said Harold to himself. 'But Hilda is older than I, and Hector is younger, so I think I will go out too.' So he ran after the others, and came up with them just as Hector had picked up the black ball and was tossing it to Hilda.

'Let us play in a triangle,' said Harold. So they stood at the three corners, and tossed the ball from one to another.

But, strange to say, the wind, which had been blowing all day from the south, had suddenly changed to the north; and the spots on the children's faces began to get blacker than ink and hotter than pepper. And, as they had to keep rubbing the spots first with one hand and then with another, they were continually missing the ball when

it was thrown to them; and they did not
notice that every time it fell to the ground it
struck nearer and nearer to the tall hedge
which divided Rumpty-Dudget's land from
the Queen's. At last Harold got the ball to
himself, and kept tossing it up and down
without letting the others have their turn.
Hereupon Hilda and Hector began to run
after him to take the ball away from him; but
just as they caught up with him he gave the
ball a great throw, and it flew clear over the
high hedge, and came down with a bounce in
Rumpty-Dudget's garden. It wanted three
minutes to sunset.

The three children were a good deal
frightened at this, and looked at one another
in dismay. But they did not yet know how
much reason for fright there was.

'It is your fault!' said Hector to Harold.

'It is your fault!' said Harold to Hilda.

'It is your fault!' said Hilda to Hector.

'Let us look through the hole in the
hedge,' said Hector, putting his finger on his
chin, where the black spot was. Hilda put
her finger upon the spot on her forehead
and followed him; and Harold followed them

both, with his finger on his nose.   They came
to the hole in the hedge, and looked through
it.

‘I can see it!’ exclaimed Hilda.

‘It is not far off,’ said Harold.   ‘If the
north wind did not blow so hard through this
hole we might jump through and get it.’

‘I don’t mind jumping against the north
wind,’ said Hector boldly; and with that he
jumped through the hole : and the sun set.

‘It is too late!’ said Tom the Cat, who
appeared between Harold and Hilda at that
moment.   ‘I cannot save him now.   Look!’

Hector, after jumping through the hedge,
had run up to the black ball and stooped to
pick it up.   But the ball moved and unfolded
itself, and a little cackling laugh came out of
it, and it stood up on its legs.   It was no
other than Rumpty-Dudget himself.

‘Now, my young prince, you will come
with me and stand in my hundred-and-first
corner!’ said he, with a malignant grin.

‘No, I won’t!’ said Hector.

At that Rumpty-Dudget took a piece of
black string from his pocket and held one end
of it to the black spot on Hector’s chin ; and
it stuck to it so fast that all the pulling in the

world could not pull it off. Then Rumpty-Dudget put the string over his shoulder, and so dragged Hector into his tower, and put him in the hundred-and-first corner.

As soon as this was done the north wind increased to a hurricane ; the beautiful palace was blown away, the Garden of Delight was destroyed, and nothing was left but a desert covered with grey stones and brambles. The dull grey cloud covered all the sky, and Rumpty-Dudget was master of the whole country.

CHAPTER IV.

NO TIME TO BE LOST.

PRINCESS HILDA and Prince Harold sat down on a heap of rubbish that happened to be near them, and cried heartily. Tom the Cat sat before them, moving the end of his tail first one way and then the other, and looking very sorrowful out of his yellow eyes. But presently he said :

'Crying will not get poor Hector back again.'

'Can we ever get him back ?' sobbed Harold.

' I would do anything !' whimpered Hilda.

' If our Fairy Aunt were only here,' said Harold, 'perhaps she could tell us what we ought to do.'

'You will not see the Fairy Aunt again,' Tom replied, 'until you have got Hector out of the grey tower, where he is at this moment standing, with his face to the wall and his

hands behind his back, in the one-hundred-
and-first corner.'

'But what can we do?' cried Hilda, beginning to weep afresh. 'We are nothing
but little children.'

'Perhaps you may be able to do more than
if you were grown up,' Tom replied. 'It depends a good deal upon how much you love
Hector.'

'Oh!' exclaimed both the children at
once; and as they could not think of anything
big enough to compare their love for Hector
to, they said nothing more.

'Listen to me, then,' said Tom, 'and all
may yet be well. But in the first place get on
my back, so that I may take you out of this
desert and into the great forest, where we can
lay our plans without being interrupted.'

So saying Tom rose and curved his back:
the two children jumped upon it; off they all
went, and, in less time than it takes to tell
it, they were in the midst of that great Forest
of Mystery which they had so often seen from
the window of their chamber, but which, until
now, they had never entered. It was quite
still, except a faint chopping noise that seemed
to come from a long way off.

'What makes that noise?' Hilda asked.

'That is Rumpty-Dudget cutting down
the trees,' Tom replied; 'and unless we can
stop him he will cut down every one of them.
However, he will hardly get so far as this to-
night.   Now, children, sit down and listen.'

The children accordingly seated themselves on a cushion of moss at the foot of one
of the tallest pine-trees in the forest, and the
cat sat down in front of them, with his thick
tail curled round his toes.

'The first thing to be done,' said Tom,
looking at the children with his yellow eyes,
which burned as brightly as lamps in the
gloom of the forest, 'the first thing to be done
is, of course, to get the Golden Ivy-seed and
the Diamond Waterdrop.   After that the
rest is easy.'

'And where are the Golden Ivy-seed and
the Diamond Waterdrop to be found?' inquired the two children hopefully.

'The Golden Ivy-seed must be sought in
the centre of the earth, where the King of
the Gnomes reigns,' replied the cat; 'and the
Diamond Waterdrop is to be asked for in the
kingdom of the Air Spirits, above the clouds.'

'But how are we to get up to the Air

Spirits and down to the Gnomes?' asked the children disconsolately.

'We will see about that,' replied the cat. 'But before starting we must build the en-chanted bonfire.'

'What good will that do?' demanded the children.

'We could never get on without it,' re-plied Tom. 'For since Hector has been put into the one-hundred-and-first corner the sun has caught fire and the moon has frozen up, and this fire will be all we can have to warm and light us on our journey.'

'But what if it should go out while we are away?' said the children.

'In order to prevent that one of you must stay by it, while the other goes with me on the journey,' said Tom. 'Harold, you shall be the one to stay. Be sure and not let the fire go out whatever happens; for if it does, Rumpty-Dudget will take the blackened logs and rub Hector's face all over with them, and then we should never be able to get him out of the tower at all. Now do you two run about and pick up all the dried sticks you can find, and pile them together in a heap, while I get the touchwood ready.'

'In a few minutes—so diligently did Hilda and Harold work—a heap of faggots had been gathered together as high as the top of Hilda's head. Meanwhile Tom the Cat had not been idle. He had drawn on the ground with the tip of his tail a large circle, in the centre of which was the heap of faggots. It had now become quite dark, and the children could not have seen their way about had it not been for Tom's yellow eyes, which burned as brightly as two carriage-lamps.

'Come inside the circle, children,' said he at length. 'I am now going to light the touchwood.'

In they came accordingly, and sat down again on the moss cushion at the foot of the tall pine-tree. The cat then put the touch-wood on the ground and crouched down in front of it, with his nose resting against it; and he stared and stared at it with his flaming yellow eyes, and by and by it began to smoke and smoulder, and at last it caught fire and burned away famously.

'That will do nicely,' said the cat; 'now put on some sticks.'

Hilda and Harold heaped on the dry sticks in handfuls; and so the enchanted fire was fairly started, and it burned blue, red, and yellow.

'And now there is no time to be lost,' said Tom the Cat. 'Harold, you will stay beside this fire, and keep it burning until I come back with Hilda from the kingdoms of the Air Spirits and of the Gnomes. Remember, that if you let the fire go out it can never again be lighted, and all will be lost. Nevertheless, you must on no account go outside the circle to gather more faggots, if those which are already inside get used up before we return. You may, perhaps, be tempted to do so; but if you yield to the temptation all will go wrong. Your brother Hector will then be in greater danger than ever, and the only way you can save him will be to get into the fire yourself and burn!'

Prince Harold did not much like the idea of being left alone in the woods all night, with the sound of Rumpty-Dudget's axe coming ever nearer and nearer. Still, since it was for his little brother Hector's sake, he never dreamed of refusing. But he made up his mind to be particularly careful not to use up the faggots too fast, so that he would not be tempted to go outside the ring.

Hilda and Tom kissed him, and bade him farewell ; then Hilda got on the cat's back, and nestled down amidst the warm white fur. Tom sprang on to the trunk of the tall pine-tree, and away ! straight upwards they went, and were out of sight in the twinkling of an eye.

CHAPTER V.

AFTER climbing upwards for a long time they came at last to the very tiptop of the pine-tree, which was just on a level with the upper surface of the clouds.

'We are now above the reach of the north wind,' remarked the cat; 'and this is the only tree in the forest tall enough for our purpose. All the clouds hereabouts, as you see, are blown by the south wind and by the west. If we rode on one blown by the north we should be driven straight into Rumpty-Dudget's power.'

'Are we going to ride on a cloud, then?' asked Hilda, feeling a little nervous; for it was a terrible distance if they should fall.

'Hold tight to me, and you will be safe,' replied Tom. 'Here comes the cloud we want—it will pass within two yards of us. As we make the jump do you look down to

M

the foot of the tree and see whether Harold
is in his place and the fire still burning.'

Hardly had Tom done speaking, when
the cloud sailed by, passing, as he had said,
within two yards of the top of the pine-tree
to which they were clinging. The cat jumped,
and alighted very cleverly on the cloud's
edge, and a moment's scramble brought them
to the top. Meanwhile, Hilda had looked
downward to the foot of the tree as they
took their leap; and she had caught a
glimpse of Harold sitting within the ring,
beside the enchanted fire, and seeming rather disconsolate. But the fire was burning
brightly, yellow, red, and blue.

The cloud sailed away, and took them
to a part of the sky which Hilda had never
seen before. It was full of a strange white
light, and no darkness ever came there. On
went the cloud, moving slowly but steadily,
like a great ship steering its way amidst the
sky. The kingdom of the Air Spirits soon
loomed in sight. Rainbow bridges spanned
its shining rivers; its forests were like the
tracery of the Northern Lights; and the
houses and palaces in which the people lived
were stars of different sizes, along whose
rays was the only path to get to them.

At length the cloud entered the harbour, and, letting down an anchor of raindrops, its motion ceased.

'You must go the rest of the way alone, Hilda,' said the cat. 'I shall wait for you, and you will find me here on your return.'

'But which way am I to go, and what am I to do?' asked Hilda in a tremulous tone; for being so high above the earth almost took her breath away.

'You must ask the first Air Spirit you meet to show you the star where the Queen lives, and then you must get there the best way you can,' Tom replied. 'When you have found her you must ask her for the Diamond Waterdrop. But be very careful not to sit down, however much you may be tempted to do so; for if you do, your little brother Hector never can be saved.'

Hilda did not much like the idea of making so perilous a journey as this promised to be, without even the cat to go with her; but since it was for Hector's sake she never dreamed of refusing: only she made up her mind on no account to sit down, no matter what happened. She bade Tom farewell, therefore, and walked off.

She had not gone far when she met an Air Spirit, carrying its nose in the air—as, of course, all Air Spirits do.

'Can you tell me which star the Queen sits in?' Hilda asked.

'What do you want of the Queen?' inquired the Air Spirit superciliously.

'I want to ask her where the Diamond Waterdrop is,' answered Hilda.

'You will never get on in this country unless you carry your nose more in the air than you do,' observed the Air Spirit. 'As for her Majesty, she sits in the large star up yonder with the white ray. Mind you don't break your neck. Ta-ta!'

Hilda went onward very disconsolately. As to carrying her nose in the air she had never in her life felt less inclined to do such a thing. By and by she came to the spot where the white ray of light from the Queen's star touched the solid air. A number of Air Spirits were walking up and down it like so many tight-rope dancers.

'Look at that absurd child!' they said to one another. 'See how she hangs her head! Why doesn't she put on airs? She will never come to anything.'

Hilda began to climb up the long white ray; and though at first she was very much frightened, by degrees she gained courage, and at last she was able to walk along tolerably fast. But it was a long distance to the top, and by the time she got there she was almost ready to drop with fatigue.

The star, when she entered it, was a glorious place indeed; and the Queen of the Air Spirits was dazzlingly beautiful, though Hilda fancied that she looked upon her rather haughtily. She was seated upon a throne of fretted sunshine; and as soon as Hilda was within hearing she said:

'I have been expecting you. You have come a long way, and you look very tired. Come here and sit down.'

'No, your Majesty,' replied Hilda faintly, 'I have no time to sit down or to stay. I have come to ask you for the Diamond Waterdrop.'

'For the Diamond Waterdrop indeed!' exclaimed the Queen, laughing. 'And pray what made you suppose that you would find the Diamond Waterdrop here? However, sit down here beside me, and let us talk about it. Such a question as you ask cannot be answered in a moment.'

But Hilda shook her head.

' Listen to me, my dear Princess,' said the Queen again, more courteously than she had yet spoken. ' I know that you like to have everything your own way ; and, as you are perhaps aware, there is no one who can have things so entirely her own way as can the Queen of the Air Spirits. Now, Princess Hilda, if you will sit down here on my throne I will let you be Queen of the Air Spirits instead of me. You shall have everything your own way, and you shall put on as many airs as you please. Come !'

When Hilda heard this she certainly felt for a moment very much tempted to do as the Queen asked her. But the next moment the thought came to her of her poor little brother Hector, standing in the hundred-and-first corner of Rumpty-Dudget's tower, with his face to the wall and his hands behind his back. So she answered, with tears in her eyes :

' Oh, Queen of the Air Spirits, I am so sorry for my little brother that I do not any longer care to have everything my own way, or to put on airs, or to do anything except find the Diamond Waterdrop, so that Hector may be saved. Can you tell me where it is ?'

But the Queen shook her beautiful head and frowned.

'I have no Diamond Waterdrop,' said she. 'Ask yourself where it is.'

Then poor Hilda felt as if her heart would break, and she sobbed out :

'Oh, what shall I do to save my poor little brother ?'

There was no answer, and Hilda turned away. But, as she did so, the Queen suddenly said :

'I see the Diamond Waterdrop now, Hilda !'

'Oh, where ?' cried Hilda, turning again eagerly.

The Queen was smiling upon her now with a very kind expression.

'It is on your own cheek !' said she.

Hilda was so bewildered that, at first, she could only gaze at the Queen without moving or speaking.

'Yes,' the Queen continued, in a gentle tone, 'you might have searched through all the kingdoms of the earth and air, and yet

never have found that precious Diamond,
had you not loved your brother Hector more
than you loved to be Queen. That tear upon
your cheek, Hilda, which you shed for love
of him, is the Diamond Waterdrop that you
have sought. Keep it in this crystal phial;
be prudent, patient, and resolute, and sooner
or later Hector will be free.'

As the Queen spoke she held out a small
crystal phial, and the tear from Hilda's cheek
fell into it. Then the Queen hung the phial
about Hilda's neck by a chain of moon-
sparkles, and kissed her tenderly and bade
her farewell. And away went Hilda, light of
foot, for the weariness had left her. But as
she went she kept fancying that she had
somewhere heard a voice like this Queen's
before; but where or when she could not
tell.

She now reached the solid air again, and
hastening her steps, she presently arrived at
the harbour in which the cloud was anchored;
and there she found Tom the Cat awaiting
her. He got up and stretched himself as she
approached; and when he saw the crystal
phial hanging at her neck by its chain of
moon-sparkles he said:

' So far all has gone well. But the hardest part is yet to-come : we have to find the Golden Ivy-seed. There is no time to be lost, so jump on my back, and let us be off ! '

With that he curved his back, Hilda put her arms round his neck and nestled down in the soft white fur, and Tom gave a great leap off the edge of the cloud, and away! down they went through the empty air like a live snowball, and it seemed to Hilda that they never would have done falling. At length, however, they alighted safely on the top of a haystack, and the next moment they were standing in the hayfield.

CHAPTER VI.

THE KING OF THE GNOMES.

JUST beside the haystack was a field-mouse's
hole, or what looked like one ; and something
that looked like a little brown mouse, but
which might have been something else for
all Hilda could tell, was sitting at the entrance
of it.   But when it saw the cat it rose up on
its little hind legs, turned a complete somersault, and then darted away down the hole ;
and Hilda noticed that it had no tail.

'What a curious mouse!' she said to
Tom.

'It was a Gnome,' he replied : 'they are
often mistaken for mice when they appear on
the surface of the ground.'

'Where has he gone to?' inquired Hilda.

'Down to the centre of the earth, to be
sure,' said Tom, 'to tell the others that we
are coming.'

'But we can never get into such a little hole as that,' Hilda said.

'Get on my back, and hold fast!' was all Tom's answer; and when Hilda had nestled down in his soft white fur and clasped her arms round his neck he began scratching at the hole with both his fore-paws, and throwing up the dirt in a mighty heap behind; till in a wonderfully short time a large passage was made, opening towards the centre of the earth.

'Hold fast!' said Tom again, and into the passage they went.

If it had not been for the cat's eyes, which shone like two yellow carriage-lamps, they might more than once have missed their way, for it was as dark as pitch during the first part of the journey. Hilda, as she clung close to the cat's back, could see that they were passing rapidly through what seemed to be a series of caves, one opening into another, and growing always higher and broader as they went on. At first the air felt damp and cold; but as they sped onwards it grew warmer and drier; and now the wall of the caverns began to throw back gleams of many-coloured light, as if from gigantic jewels sticking there; and

presently the light increased, without seeming
to come from anywhere in particular; and the
great vault overhead seemed to soar aloft,
until only a misty brightness was visible, like
the sky at sunset-time, when it is feathered
with gorgeous clouds. It was a new and
marvellous country, with gold and silver fila-
gree instead of foliage, and fields of emerald,
and rivers of sapphires, and distant mountains
of amethyst. By and by the cat came to two
lofty pillars of plain white alabaster, and there
he stopped.

'Now, Hilda,' he said, 'you must go the
rest of the way alone. Pass between those
pillars, and then you will be in the kingdom
of the Gnomes. Ask the first Gnome you
meet to show you the place where the King
ploughs; and when you have found him, ask
him where the Golden Ivy-seed is. But be
very careful to do everything that he bids
you, no matter how strange or disagreeable it
may be; for, if you disobey him, your brother
Hector cannot be saved.'

Though Hilda did not much like the idea
of going on through this strange land all by
herself, still, since it was for Hector's sake,
she never dreamed of refusing; only she made
up her mind to do everything the King bade

her, whatever happened. So off she started,
and after passing between the alabaster pillars
she came to a road on which the gold-dust lay
an inch thick; for it seldom rains in the centre
of the earth. Pretty soon she met a little
brown Gnome, running along on all-fours, and
turning somersaults, as all Gnomes do.

'Will you show me the place where the
King ploughs?' asked Hilda.

'What do you want of him?' asked the
Gnome.

'I want to ask him to tell me where the
Golden Ivy-seed is,' Hilda replied.

'He ploughs in the emerald field on the
other side of the mountain of amethyst,' said
the Gnome; 'but, unless you can go on all-
fours and turn somersaults better than you
seem able to do, you will never get on in this
country.'

But Hilda had never walked on all-fours,
much less turned somersaults, since she was
a baby a year old; so she trudged along the
dusty golden road just as she was, and all the
Gnomes who met her threw somersaults and
said:

'See how upright she walks! She will
never come to anything!'

The road was very long, the amethyst

mountain was very far away, and Hilda was very tired by the time she arrived at the emerald field. But there was the field at last, and there was the King of the Gnomes on all-fours in the midst of it. He was a strange little being, with piercing black eyes, immensely broad shoulders, and a beard of white asbestos woven together like a woman's braid. As soon as he caught sight of Hilda he shouted out to her :

'Get down on all-fours this instant! How dare you come into my kingdom walking upright?'

Hilda was a good deal frightened at the way the King spoke ; but she answered resolutely, 'Your Majesty, I walked upright because there was no time to lose, and I have come to ask you for the Golden Ivy-seed.'

'The Golden Ivy-seed, forsooth!' exclaimed the King, with a deep laugh. 'What made you suppose, I should like to know, that there was any Golden Ivy-seed to be got here? The Golden Ivy-seed is not given to people with stiff necks, I can assure you ; so get down on all-fours at once, or else go about your business.'

Then Hilda remembered what Tom the

Cat had told her, and down she dropped on all-fours without a word.

'Now, listen to me,' said the King sternly. 'I shall harness you to that plough in the place of my horses, and you must drag it up and down over this field until the whole of it is ploughed, while I follow behind with the whip. Hitch yourself to the shaft immediately. Come!'

When Hilda heard this command it seemed to her at first as if it was impossible that she could obey it. For she was weary with her long journey along the golden road and over the mountain of amethyst, and the King's plough looked very heavy, and his whip very long; and, besides, she thought it was much beneath the dignity of a princess such as she was to be driven on all-fours through a ploughed field. But the next moment the thought came to her of her poor little brother Hector, standing in the hundred-and-first corner of Rumpty-Dudget's tower, with his face to the wall and his hands behind his back. So she said humbly:

'Oh, King of the Gnomes! I am so sorry for my brother Hector that for his sake I will do as you bid me, in the hope that afterwards

you will tell me where the Golden Ivy-seed
is to be found, so that Hector may be saved
from Rumpty-Dudget's tower.'

The King made no reply whatever, but
he harnessed Hilda to the plough, and she
dragged it back and forth across the emerald
field until the whole of it was ploughed, while
the King followed behind with the whip. At
last he unharnessed her.

'Now begone about your business!' he
said roughly.

'But you have not told me where the
Golden Ivy-seed is,' said Hilda, with a piteous
throb in her heart.

'I have no Golden Ivy-seed!' returned
the King, with his deep laugh. 'Why don't
you ask yourself where it is?'

At this poor Hilda's heart felt as if it were
broken, and she sank down on the ground and
sobbed out:

'Oh! what shall I do to save my little
brother?'

But hereupon the King of the Gnomes
smiled upon her, and he said, in a gentler
voice than he had yet used:

'Put your hand to your heart, Hilda, and
see what you find there.'

Hilda did not understand what he meant;

but she had by this time got so used to obey-
ing him that she put her hand to her heart,
and felt something fall into the palm of her
hand ; and when in astonishment she looked
at it, behold, it was a tiny golden seed !

'Yes,' said the King kindly, 'you might
have searched through all the kingdoms of
the earth and air, and yet never have found
that precious seed, had not your heart been
broken like this field for love of your brother
Hector. Keep the Golden Ivy-seed in this
hollow pearl ; be humble, patient, and gentle,
and sooner or later Hector will be free.'

As he said these words he fastened the
pearl to her girdle with a jewelled clasp, and
kissed her on the forehead and bade her farewell. And as Hilda trudged back along the
golden road and over the mountain of amethyst she kept thinking that somewhere she
had heard a voice like this King's before ; but
where or when she could not tell.

In course of time she arrived at the alabaster pillars, and, passing out between them,
she found Tom the Cat awaiting her. He got
up and stretched himself as she approached ;
and when he saw the hollow pearl at her
girdle he said :

N

'So far all has gone well. But now we must see whether or not Harold has kept the enchanted fire going. There is no time to be lost; so jump on my back and hold fast, and let us be off.'

With that he curved his back; Hilda clasped her arms round his neck as before, and away they went, through the gleaming caverns, and up the sombre passages, and through the cold damp tunnels, until at last out they popped beside the haystack in the field; and after they had come out the little brown creature which had been sitting waiting at the entrance threw a somersault into the great pit and disappeared. And immediately the whole heap of earth which Tom had dug up fell back into its place, and nothing was left but a small round crevice in the ground, like a field-mouse's hole.

CHAPTER VII.

THE ENCHANTED FIRE.

Now, Harold—after he had seen Hilda and the cat vanish up the trunk of the tall pine-tree—had sat himself down rather disconsolately beside the fire, which was blazing away famously, yellow, red, and blue. He rested his back against the trunk of the tree, and fixed his eyes upon the fire; it made a slight rustling and crackling noise as it burned. There was also another noise, but that did not come from the fire; it was a chopping noise, sounding far away in the forest, and Harold knew that it was Rumpty-Dudget cutting down the trees. Each time he heard this sound it seemed to be a little nearer. Then he would wonder to himself what he should do if Rumpty-Dudget were suddenly to appear. He must not, at all events, let the fire go out; and every once in a while he took a faggot from the pile that he and Hilda had heaped

N 2

up and put it in the leaping flame; but he
was very careful to avoid stepping outside the
circle which Tom the Cat had drawn with the
tip of his tail.

In this manner a very long time passed
away, and Harold, who had never sat up so
late before in his life, began to get uncommonly sleepy. But still Hilda and Tom did
not return; and Harold knew that, if he were
to lie down and take a nap, the enchanted fire
might go out before he waked up again; and,
as Tom had warned him, once out it could
never be rekindled. Moreover, Rumpty-
Dudget would then be able to steal the fire-
blackened logs and blacken poor Hector's
face all over with them, so that he never
could be saved. Therefore Harold kept
himself awake, partly by sitting on a pine-
needle which he had found stuck in the moss
cushion, and partly by putting fresh faggots
into the flame, which went on burning blue,
yellow, and red.

But another very long time passed away,
and the sound of Rumpty-Dudget's axe
sounded nearer, and the forest was dark and
full of mystery, and there was no sign yet of
Hilda and the cat. 'I never knew before,'

said Harold to himself, 'that a night was so much longer than a day. I always thought they were a great deal shorter. But then I have no Fairy Aunt now to come and whisper pleasant stories into my ear. Heigho! well, I suppose I must put on another faggot.' And he got up to fetch one.

Much to his consternation, however, he found that there was now only a single faggot left of all those that he and Hilda had gathered together.

He was really frightened at this, and knew not what to do ; for this last faggot would soon be burnt up, and then what was to be done to keep the enchanted fire going ? He made a careful search inside the ring, and satisfied himself that there was not so much as another chip to be found there ; and Tom had told him that if he went outside the ring all would be lost.

However, the last faggot was not gone yet, and in order to make it last as long as possible Harold took it apart and put only one stick at a time on the fire ; but it was alarming to see how quickly the flame ate up one after another, and seemed hungrier than ever. After a while all but the last stick was gone. A

little while more and that had to be put in
too. And then Prince Harold sat down quite
in despair and cried with all his might. He
was at the end of everything, and at his wit's
end too.

At that moment he heard a voice calling
to him; and looking up he saw an odd little
man standing just outside the circle, carrying
a great bundle of faggots on his shoulder.
Harold's eyes were so full of tears that he did
not see that this odd little man was Rumpty-
Dudget himself; or else (what is quite as
likely) the dwarf had some spell by means of
which he could make himself appear different
from what he was.

'What are you crying for, my poor dear
little boy?' asked Rumpty-Dudget of Prince
Harold in his most coaxing voice.

'Because I have used up all my faggots,'
he answered.

'Used them all up! But surely there are
plenty more in the forest where those came
from?' the dwarf answered in pretended surprise. 'Besides, what harm if the fire does
go out? It isn't a cold night, and the moon
will be up presently.'

'But if the fire goes out,' said Harold, 'my
poor little brother Hector cannot be saved.'

'Oh, that is the trouble, is it?' exclaimed the dwarf. 'Well, now, it is lucky I happened to come along this way; you could not have met with a better adviser than I am. For I know all about this Rumpty-Dudget, with whom your brother Hector is staying; and I saw Hector myself not an hour ago.'

'Oh! did you?' cried Harold in great excitement.

'To be sure I did; and very well he looked, I can tell you. He has done nothing but eat sugar-candy and blow on a tin whistle ever since he went there; and he says he wants nothing better than to stay with Rumpty-Dudget all his life. And, by the way, he asked me to tell you if I saw you that he hoped you and your sister would come and join; for that Rumpty-Dudget is the pleasantest fellow in the world, and not at all like what you had been made to believe him.'

'Oh-h!' exclaimed Harold, staring at Rumpty-Dudget with wide-open eyes. 'I don't see how that can be true. Who are you?'

'A friend,' replied Rumpty-Dudget. 'And to prove it I have brought over this bundle of faggots; and when these are used up I will get you some more.'

'Oh, thank you very much!' exclaimed Harold, jumping for joy, and going as near to the inside edge of the circle as he could. 'Give them to me quick, for there is no time to be lost; the fire is just going out.'

'I can't bring them inside the circle,' said the dwarf, suddenly putting the bundle on the ground, and pretending to be very much exhausted. 'I have carried them already all the way from the further side of the forest, and that is far enough. Surely you can come the rest of the way for them yourself.'

'But I must not come outside the circle, you know,' said Harold, dancing up and down with impatience.

'Why not?'

'Because Tom the Cat said that if I did all would go wrong.'

'Pshaw! what should a cat know about a thing like this?' demanded the dwarf very scornfully. 'At all events, your fire will burn less than a minute longer; and you know what will happen when it goes out.'

At that Harold became almost beside himself with anxiety and bewilderment, and what to do he could not tell. But at last he thought that anything would be better than to let the fire go out ; so he put one foot outside the circle and stretched forth his hand for the faggots.

'Just the least bit further,' said the dwarf coaxingly. 'I would save you the trouble if I could ; but I am really too tired to stir.'

Harold saw that by stretching about six inches further he could reach a faggot. But in order to stretch six inches he would be obliged to put the other foot outside the circle. 'After all, what can it matter ?' he thought. And the next moment there he was, outside !

Immediately, with a loud laugh, the dwarf flung away the faggots far into the depths of the forest ; and rushing into the circle, he began to stamp out with his feet what was left of the enchanted fire.

Then Harold recognised Rumpty-Dudget for the first time, for the spell was off him. And Harold remembered what Tom the Cat had said, and he leaped back into the circle, and as the last bit of flame flickered at the end of the stick he laid himself down upon it. Whereupon Rumpty-Dudget gave a hoarse cry and vanished ; and the enchanted fire blazed up famously, red, blue, and yellow, with poor Harold in the midst of it.

CHAPTER VIII.

THE GOLDEN IVY.

Now, or never, it was the time for Hilda and
the cat to come back.   And, sure enough, at
this very instant there was a sound like the
whistling of a blast of wind through the forest,
and a hurrying and a skurrying, and behold!
there was Tom the Cat, with Hilda on his
back.

Tom said nothing, but he sprang into the
circle, and without losing an instant he dug a
little hole in the ground with his fore paws,
throwing up the dirt in a heap behind him.
When it was finished he said :

'Open the hollow pearl, Hilda, and put
the Golden Ivy-seed in this hole ; and make
haste, for Harold is burning for Hector's sake!'

So Hilda made haste to open the hollow
pearl and to put the Golden Ivy-seed in the
hole ; and the cat spread the earth over it, and
then said :

'Now take the crystal phial, Hilda, and
pour half the Diamond Waterdrop upon the
place where the seed is planted, and the other
half upon the enchanted fire ; and make haste,
for Harold is burning for Hector's sake !'

So Hilda made haste and did what the
cat had told her to do.

When the half of the Diamond Waterdrop
fell upon the fire in which Harold had all this
while been burning the fire was immediately
put out. And there lay Harold, alive and
well, amidst the embers ; but the black spot
upon his nose was all burned away, and his
hair and eyes, which had until then been
brown, were now quite black.

So up he jumped, and he and Hilda kissed
each other heartily, for they felt as if they
had been separated for a long time.

'What has become of the black spot on
your forehead, Hilda ?' asked Harold. 'It is
not there any more.'

'Ah !' said Tom, 'that disappeared when
the King of the Gnomes kissed her. But now
make yourselves ready, children, for we are
going to take a ride to Rumpty-Dudget's
tower.'

On hearing this the young prince and

princess were greatly surprised, and looked about for the horses on which they were to ride.

But behold! the Golden Ivy-seed, watered with the Diamond Waterdrop, was already growing and sprouting with marvellous vigour and rapidity. A strong stem, with leaves of glistening gold, had pushed itself out of the earth, and was creeping along the ground towards Rumpty-Dudget's tower: hardly creeping, either, for it moved faster than a man could run. The cat helped Hilda and Harold to a seat on two of the largest leaves, while he himself clung to the stem; and so away they went through the forest merrily. As they advanced the heavy grey cloud which had overcast all the heavens since Rumpty-Dudget's rule began was rolled back like a mighty scroll; and the pure sky, lit up with the fresh sunshine of the early dawn, smiled above the mysterious forest. Then the forest too awoke to life and joyousness; the birds sang in the branches, and fragrant flowers, sparkling with dew, glowed in the happy glades with mingled tints of white, blue, and red. So on they went, carrying with them the freshness and perfume of

the morning and of spring ; and in a wonderfully short time the Golden Ivy had brought
them to the gates of Rumpty-Dudget's tower..

'Jump down now,' said Tom, 'and leave
the Golden Ivy to do the rest.'

Down they all jumped accordingly, and
stood at one side, near the castle gates. But
the Golden Ivy kept on, and threw itself across
the moat, and clambered over the portcullis,.
and forced its way into the courtyard, and
writhed along the passages and up the stair-
cases, until (in less time than it takes to write
about it) the Ivy had reached the room with
the hundred-and-one corners.   In the midst
of this room stood Rumpty-Dudget, having
fled to it for safety ; for it was defended by
enchantments which only the Golden Ivy
could have overcome.   There he stood, trembling in his shoes, as well he might ; and in
all the corners round about, with their faces
to the wall and their hands behind their backs,.
stood the poor little children that Rumpty-
Dudget had caught.

But they were not to stand there much
longer, for Rumpty-Dudget's hour had come !
He tried to run away, but the terrible Golden
Ivy ran after him and caught him, and bound

down his arms, and tied together his legs, and
clutched him around the throat, and squeezed
him round the body, and fastened its coils
upon him tighter and tighter, until all the mischief was squeezed out of him.   But, since
Rumpty-Dudget was entirely made of mischief,
when all the mischief was squeezed out of him
of course there was no Rumpty-Dudget left
—no, not so much as one of his shoe-buckles !

And when Rumpty-Dudget had ceased to
exist of course all the children who had been
made prisoners by his spells became free ; and
they came racing and shouting out of the grey
tower, with little Prince Hector at their head.
But when Hector saw his brother and sister,
and they saw him, they all three set up a cry
of joy, and ran together and hugged and
kissed each other heartily; for they felt as if
they had been parted for a very long time.

At last Hilda said, ' Why, Hector, what
has become of the black spot that used to be
on your chin ?   It is not there any more.'

' It got rubbed off against the wall of the
room with the hundred-and-one corners,' replied Hector demurely.

At that they all three laughed ; but Hilda
at least had tears in her eyes.

'And look at his hair and eyes!' exclaimed Harold; 'they are brown now, instead of black, as they used to be. What is the reason of that?'

'It is the touch of the Golden Ivy,' said a voice behind them, which Hilda fancied she had heard somewhere before.

The three children looked round, and saw a lady standing beside them, dazzlingly beautiful, with a crown on her head and a smile in her eyes. They all knew her at once, though they had never seen her before except in their dreams. It was their Fairy Aunt.

'But you look very much like the Queen our mother,' said Hilda.

'And do I look like anyone besides her?' asked the lady, with a smile.

'Yes, you are like the Queen of the Air Spirits!' exclaimed Hilda; 'though you don't look so haughty as she did at first.'

'Anyone else?' asked the lady again, speaking in a very gruff tone, and drawing her eyebrows together.

'Dear me! that is the way the King of the Gnomes talked,' said Hilda, clasping her hands. 'Surely you couldn't have been him?'

'Yes, my darlings,' said the lady, sitting down and drawing the three children to her lap, 'I am the Queen, your mother; though, by Rumpty-Dudget's spells, I was obliged to leave you, and to be seen by you only in your dreams at night. And I was what seemed to you the Queen of the Air Spirits, Hilda, and the King of the Gnomes as well; because love shows itself in many forms, and works for you above and beneath, and both while you wake and while you sleep; but it is always the same love in the end, and if you love one another you will find it out at last.'

'After all,' said Hilda thoughtfully, 'I love you best as our own mamma. And you will always be our mamma, and be with us now, won't you?'

'Yes, my darlings,' answered the Queen, giving them all a hug and a kiss; 'there will be no more changes or partings, for Rumpty-Dudget and his tower are gone, and we are free.'

'But where is Tom the Cat?' cried Hector all of a sudden, looking this way and that. 'We can never be happy anywhere without him.'

'Oh, Tom has done his work, and we shall not see him any more,' said the Queen, shaking her head mysteriously.

But at this all the children looked ready to cry.

'Well, then, you shall have one more look at him,' said the Queen. She wore on her shoulders a long hooded mantle of the finest white fur. By a sudden movement she drew this mantle round her, and pulled the hood over her head and face; and behold! there sat Tom the Cat, looking as natural as possible, only that between the folds of the fur the children could see their mother's eyes laughing.

'I have often looked out at you so before now,' she said, as she threw back the hood and mantle; 'and you would have seen me as plainly as you do now, but that the spell prevented you. So, you see, we shall take what was really Tom the Cat along with us, after all.'

'Where are we going?' Harold asked.

'To our home in Fairyland,' answered the Queen.

And are we never coming back here

O

any more ?' asked Hilda, glad to go, and yet with almost a sigh.

'No, we shall never see this land again,' the Queen replied. 'It was beautiful, but all its beauty lives again in the land whither we go. And there are no Rumpty-Dudgets in that land, and no grey towers full of corners, and no prickly hedges, nor winds from the north. And all the stars of the air and jewels of the earth are in that land, only more glorious and splendid than those that Hilda saw. But why should I tell you about it, when you are going to see it all for yourselves this very day ? Are you ready ?'

'Yes!' said all the children together.

Then she folded her arms about them, and they clung to her neck, and so they seemed to rise aloft in the warm air, and float towards the south. Far beneath them lay the tops of the tallest trees; but the children felt no fear. For they were going to their home in Fairyland; and they are all three living there, with the Queen their mother, to this very day.

But Hilda's hair is golden still, and her eyes are blue.

CALLADON.

CHAPTER I.

ABRACADABRA.

IF you were to take three hoops, the second half as large round as the first, and the third half as large round as the second, and lay them on the floor one inside the other, you would have a ground-plan of the house in which Calladon lived. The outermost wall was built of brick, and had five narrow windows; the middle wall was of stone, and had also five windows; the inner wall was of the purest alabaster, and was a kind of window in itself.

In the centre of the innermost room a lamp was always burning, and the light which it gave out was so soft and penetrating that it glowed through the alabaster walls and illuminated the room outside with a pale white lustre, and some rays penetrated through the windows of this room into the outermost room of all, and there met the darkness that streamed in through the outer windows—for the house stood in that part of the world where it is night all the year round. The name of the innermost room was Abra, that of the middle room was Cada, and that of the outermost room was Bra. The whole house, therefore, was called Abracadabra.

It was a curious thing about this house, that if you were in Abra, you could see into both Cada and Bra, but, if you were in Cada, you could not see into Abra, and if you were in Bra, you could not see into either Abra or Cada. As a general thing, it is easier to see from darkness towards light than from light towards darkness. But there was probably something peculiar about this light—and, for the matter of that, about this darkness too.

As for Calladon himself, he was one of the best-behaved boys ever known, and he was not less good-looking than he was good. He was a fine, straight-backed, rosy-cheeked little fellow, with bright eyes, a cheerful voice, and an obedient spirit. He was seven years old, and knew as much as it is well for a boy of his age to know. This was due to the Master who had charge of him, and who had put across his breast the gold sash, which always pressed against his heart when he wished to do wrong, and reminded him to stop. The Master had lived with Calladon ever since Calladon could remember, and probably for a good while before that. The Master had tended him in his illness, played with him in his plays, helped him in his studies, and sympathised with him in his troubles. Calladon loved the Master as much as if he had been his father and mother in one. Who his father and mother might be, he, however, did not know; but the Master used to tell him that when his education was finished he should see them.

Meantime he was obliged to live in Abracadabra, and make the best of it. The only one of the three rooms which he had ever dwelt in, was the central one, Abra; but there was plenty of entertainment to be had there. In the first place, there was the lamp, which lit up not the room only, but Calladon's mind likewise, so that the more it shone upon him, the better he understood his studies. And the lamp was warm as well as bright; so warm, that not only did it make the room comfortable, but it warmed Calladon's heart likewise, and made him loving and generous. In the ceiling of the room a large ball of crystal was hung on a sort of pivot, on which it could be turned at pleasure. This crystal ball had the power of reflecting all the places best worth seeing in the world, and casting the reflections on a white disc arranged for the purpose underneath. It was by this means that Calladon had studied geography, and he had enjoyed the study more than most boys do. At other times, the ball would bring the images of the stars on the disc, so that you would have thought you were aloft in the sky, watching all the myriad worlds of light, and their movements. It may be imagined, therefore, that although Abra did not appear to be a large room, yet it must have been larger than it looked, since it was able to contain within itself the whole earth and heaven. Beyond doubt, Abra was a wonderful place, which everybody ought to see at some time of their lives. The air you breathed there had a delicate but powerful fragrance, as if it were life itself; and strangely beautiful chords of music sounded ever and anon through the room, coming from no visible instrument, but seeming to arise from the harmony and happiness in the heart of him who listened to it. Moreover, although there was not much furniture in the room, nor many toys to play with, yet whenever Calladon needed anything, he was sure to find it ready to his hand. It is true that he seldom wished for anything that he ought not to have, and if he did, the pressure of the golden sash across his heart warned him to forbear. In short, nothing could be more delightful and satisfactory than were all the arrangements in Abra; and, up to the time he was seven years old, Calladon had never wished for anything that it could not give him.

Sometimes he would amuse himself with looking through the alabaster walls into the outer rooms, Cada and Bra. These had a beauty of their own, but it was easy to see that they were less beautiful than Abra. The best use of them was, perhaps, to let it be known that Abra was better than they. Calladon once asked the Master about this, and he answered :

'If it were not for Abra, there could be no Cada, and no Bra. But neither could there be any Abra, if Cada and Bra did not surround it. The alabaster wall would burst asunder, and the flame of the lamp would burn up the world.'

'Where did the lamp come from ?' asked Calladon.

'It was here before Abracadabra or the world existed,' the Master replied, smiling ; 'and it will burn for ever.'

'Could not I put it out ?'

'No; but you might wander away from it into the darkness outside,' said the Master, in a graver tone.

'But then could I not light a little lamp of my own, to see my way about ?' Calladon inquired.

'Yes, you might do so,' the Master replied. 'But such a lamp would in time burn out, and then you could never again relight it, and you would be lost.'

'I should not like that !' exclaimed Calladon. But after a while he added, 'Still I do not understand why those two other rooms should be there, since I never go into them.'

'You live in them, even though you do not go into them,' the Master answered. 'If you did go into them, you would not live in them so much as you do now, because you could not take the light of the lamp with you.'

Calladon said nothing more, but he became thoughtful.

CHAPTER II.

THE LAW OF THE LAMP.

ONE morning, soon after Calladon's seventh birthday, the Master called him to him and said :

'My dear Calladon, you have now arrived at the age when I must leave you for awhile, to think your own thoughts, and do your own deeds. I am going away, and it is uncertain when I may come back. Before I go I shall tell you a few things which I hope you will remember.'

'But I should like to go with you,' said Calladon.

'That may come to pass hereafter,' the Master replied, 'but not now, and it will depend upon what you do and think while I am parted from you, whether or not it comes to pass at all.'

'What is it that I must do?' inquired Calladon.

' I cannot command you either to do or not to do anything,' the Master said, 'for I shall not be here to enforce obedience. But I have already taught you many things, and, if you have studied them with your whole heart and mind, they will direct you as well as I could direct you myself. All I shall do, therefore, is to tell you what you had best avoid doing, and then leave you to follow my advice or not, as you choose.'

' Oh, there will be no trouble about that!' exclaimed Calladon cheerfully, ' for will not my golden sash press against my heart whenever I go wrong, and remind me to turn back ? '

' No, for you will not wear the golden sash any more,' replied the Master. 'You are no longer a little child, and you must no longer depend on what touches your heart from the outside, but on what moves it from within.'

'Well, I think I shall like that better, on the whole,' said Calladon. 'It will make me feel more like a man. But what is it that I ought not to do, dear Master ? '

' You ought not to lose faith in the lamp,' answered the Master, ' for it gives you all you have, and all you are. And you ought not to leave Abra, for Abra only is Abracadabra. And you ought not to light a lamp of your own, for it would lead you into darkness.'

' Is that all ? ' asked Calladon.

' That is all I need tell you now,' said the Master ; 'for if you obey these three rules, you will not need to know more, and if you disobey them, nothing more that I could say would help you.'

' I would have done all that without being told,' said Calladon ; 'and the only thing I don't like is having nobody to see or to speak to.'

' I have taken care about that,' replied the Master, with a smile, 'and you will not be left entirely alone. When you wake up to-morrow morning, you will find a little girl beside you. She is to be your playmate and companion. She can help you to be happier and better than you have ever been before ; but she can also make you worse and more miserable than if you were left by yourself. It will be according as you treat her.'

' Perhaps I had better not have her,' said Calladon.

' You must run the risk ; for without risk

nothing that is really good can be got,' replied the Master. 'She will not suggest either good or evil to you ; but if your thoughts are good she will know it, and will help you to carry them out ; and if your thoughts are evil, she will think evil too, and will give you the means of doing it.'

'Does she know all this ?' Calladon asked.

'She will know nothing except from you, and as long as you are obedient to what I have told you, she will be obedient to you. But if you become disobedient, she will sooner or later begin to rule you ; and whenever that happens you will be sure to suffer.'

'Then it all depends on me ?' said Calladon.

'If harm comes, you will have no right to blame her,' the Master answered ; 'but if good comes, you will have no right to take the credit to yourself.'

'Well,' said Calladon, after thinking awhile, 'the safest thing will be not to think of myself at all.'

'There is one thing more,' said the Master, before taking leave of him. 'You will find, hanging round Callia's neck (Callia is the name of your playmate), a little mirror, set in a frame of precious stones. This mirror will always show you an image of yourself, not as you think yourself to be, but as you really are. If you trust to what the mirror tells you, you will not know trouble ; but if you disregard it, you will be in danger. The mirror is the only thing that will always tell you the truth.'

'I will always believe it,' said Calladon ; and then the Master bade him good night, and Calladon fell asleep.

CHAPTER III.

CALLIA AND THE MIRROR.

THE next morning, when Calladon woke up, the first thing he saw was a lovely little girl slumbering beside him.

For a moment he was greatly astonished, for he had forgotten that the Master had gone, and that he had promised him a companion. But presently the memory of the day before came back to him, and he recollected that henceforth he was to take care of himself. The thought made him feel quite brave and manly ; and with such a beautiful playmate as this to keep him company, he felt sure that he would be the happiest boy in the world. And as he wanted his happiness, and hers, to begin as soon as possible, he bent over and kissed her on the lips.

She opened a pair of lovely blue eyes, and yawned, and said—

'Where am I ? Oh ! Calladon, is that

you? How handsome you look, and how good you are!'

'How did you know me?' asked Calladon.

'If I am Callia, you must be Calladon!' replied she, laughing. Who else could you be?'

'Now that I look in your eyes, it seems as if I must have always known you!' said Calladon.

'And I know you the same way,' said Callia.

'But how did you get here?' he asked.

'What a funny question! as if I had ever been anywhere else!'

'It is very strange, however,' he said; 'for though I can remember living here for a long time and not seeing you, still I cannot imagine your ever having been away from me. We seem always to have been together.'

'So we have,' replied Callia; 'and we will always stay together, won't we?'

'Indeed we will,' said Calladon; 'so now give me a kiss, and let us have our breakfast.'

Their breakfast was there waiting for them, as was everything else they needed; and while they were eating it they talked about what they would do during the day. They soon found out that the difficulty would be to make a choice from the many pleasant things that suggested themselves ; and whatever one proposed, the other declared to be more delightful than anything yet. And after all, what could be more delightful than simply to be together ? Calladon was more pleased in knowing that Callia was pleased than he could have been at anything that merely pleased himself; and his pleasure gave greater pleasure to Callia than any pleasure of her own could have done. What they did, therefore, on this first day, was not of nearly so much importance to them as that they did it together ; and when the day came to an end (as it did, more quickly than any day that either of them could remember) all they knew was that it had been one song of joy. As to doing anything that the Master had warned them against, they really had not had time so much as to think of such a thing.

But night came at last, and they found themselves getting sleepy. Before going to bed, Calladon said—

'By the way, Callia, have you got a mirror round your neck ? '

Do you mean this pretty little thing, set

in precious stones ? Shall I give it to you, dearest Calladon ? '

'Oh, no ; only the Master said that I was to look in it every once in a while, to find out what I really am.'

'You really are the handsomest and dearest boy in the world, and so the mirror will tell you,' said Callia ; and she held it up before him as she spoke. Calladon looked ; and certainly the mirror did show him the image of a very charming little face and figure. It told the truth, and the truth was very agreeable.

'I am glad of it for your sake, Callia,' said Calladon. 'I hope I shall always be as handsome as you want me to be.'

'I don't mind whether you are handsome or not, as long as you are Calladon,' she answered.

'It seems to me, Callia, that if I have you, and you have me, we do not need anything else.'

'And it would not make any difference whether we were in Abra or not.'

'I should hardly mind even if the lamp were to go out,' said Calladon.

' I only care for the lamp because it lets me see you,' she answered.

' And because it lets me see myself in the mirror.'

' Why should you believe the mirror more than me ? ' asked Callia.

' Well, if you think I am handsome, it is not so much matter whether the mirror tells me I am or not,' returned Calladon.

And with this they kissed each other, and fell asleep.

CHAPTER IV.

THE OUTER ROOMS.

WHEN they awoke next day, Calladon stretched himself, and shivered a little. The lamp seemed to be burning rather more dimly than usual, and the air seemed thin and cold. Glancing at Callia, who was lying with her eyes still half closed, his eye caught the sparkle of the mirror round her neck, and he took a peep into it. It seemed to him that his cheeks looked pale, and his eyes dull.

'Callia!' he exclaimed, 'Callia! wake up, and tell me how I look.'

'You look just the same,' answered she, opening her eyes and sitting up. 'But don't you think it is colder than it was yesterday?'

'I was sure it was; and if you feel it too, it must be so. But are you quite certain that I look as well and handsome as when you

first saw me ? because, in the mirror, I seemed
to be pale and dull.'

'The mirror must be wrong, then,' said
Callia ; 'for I can see you with my own eyes,
and of course I should know if there were
any difference.'

'Well,' said Calladon, 'I suppose it is
time we had our breakfast.'

The breakfast was there, but it was neither
so good nor so plentiful as before; and Calladon and Callia felt comparatively little appetite. This displeased them ; and they began
to ask each other how they should contrive
to amuse themselves during the day. They
proposed many things, but afterwards re-
jected them, either because they had done
them yesterday, or because they did not find
them any longer attractive.

'This is rather a small room, after all, for
two people to pass their lives in,' remarked
Calladon at last.

'Especially when there are two other
larger ones outside,' added Callia.

'It would be good fun to explore them,
wouldn't it?' said Calladon.

'Why shouldn't we do it?' asked Callia.

'It makes me feel quite lively again to

think of it,' exclaimed Calladon, springing to his feet. 'Only,' he added, 'that is one of the things the Master told us not to do.'

'Oh, I don't believe the Master would mind,' said Callia. 'Besides, how should he ever know anything about it ? He has gone away.'

'Of course, too, it is our own affair,' observed Calladon. 'If any harm comes of it, it will be to ourselves, and not to him.'

'I am not afraid,' said Callia. 'Are you ?'

'Not in the least. By the way, though, I am not sure that I know the way out of Abra. There doesn't seem to be any door.'

'I think I can find the way, if that is all,' returned Callia. 'I don't know how I happened to think of it—but since we have been talking about going, it has seemed to me that if we were to push against that little carved knob in the wall, it would open a passage into the room outside. Shall we try it ?'

'Yes,' said Calladon ; 'it can do no harm to see whether you are right, at all events.' So they went to the knob, and Calladon gave it a push.

'Not that way ; you should push it sideways ; see—like this,' said Callia ; and she shoved it a little towards the right. Sure enough, a part of the alabaster wall slid back, so that the children were able to look into the room beyond.

'It seems rather dark; don't you think so?' remarked Calladon, drawing back after a moment.

'We must take a lamp along with us,' said Callia. 'That lamp that burns in the centre of the room will be no use to us. We shan't be able to see anything without a lamp of our own.'

'Well, I suppose we must,' said Calladon. 'Now I think of it, though, that was another of the things the Master said we ought not to do.'

'What did he say would happen to us if we did do it?'

'I don't remember his saying anything.'

'Of course he didn't! because nothing will happen, except that we shall know more than we could know by staying here. He was only trying whether he could frighten you.'

'You shall see that I am not so easily frightened,' said Calladon. 'I am a man now, and able to take care of myself. Come, let us light a lamp of our own and go. I will show you the way.'

'Here is a lamp,' said Callia. 'I just found it on this little shelf in the corner, though I had not seen it there before. But how shall we light it?'

'We must light it from the great lamp; there is no other way.'

'But then it will be the light of that great lamp that will guide us, after all.'

'No,' said Calladon, 'because the part of the flame that we take away will become our own, and would keep on burning even if the great lamp were to go out.'

They lit the lamp accordingly. As they did so, the air around them grew colder than before, and a gust of strangely melancholy music sighed through the room. From the crystal ball in the roof overhead there came a red reflection, as of some terrible fire burning in the world without; and then a white flash, as if an angel's sword had suddenly been thrust down into the room. Now the sword seemed to be brandished about the great lamp, its point against the children, who shrank back in fear towards the alabaster wall. Still the sword threatened them; and there was a violent rush of icy wind, which forced them to the opening leading to the outer chamber.

For a moment they tried to struggle against it, and not to be driven from the alabaster room in which they had lived so happily; but the blast grew stronger, and the sword came nearer; and at last Callia cried out:

'Let us go, Calladon, or our light will be lost!'

'Come, then!' said he; and hand in hand they staggered through the opening, which closed behind them with a hollow sound. Then there was silence. Save for the wavering flame of their little lamp they were in darkness.

'What have you done, Callia?' said Calladon.

'It is your doing as much as mine,' she answered. 'Well, I suppose we must make the best of it. At any rate, it is not so cold here as it was in the other room.'

'No, and there is not that terrible light to dazzle our eyes. And that sword—we are safe from that!'

'I think, upon the whole, we are better off where we are; and I am glad we came,' said Callia. 'It is more mysterious here, and I like mystery. If you can see everything around you merely by opening your eyes, it is stupid. Here we have the excitement of going about and not knowing what we may find.'

'It is strange it should be so dark!' remarked Calladon. 'On which side of us is the alabaster wall? No light comes through either side; and yet, when we were in Abra, it seemed to shine through and illuminate both the outer rooms.'

'The great lamp must have gone out; all lamps go out after a while, I suppose,' replied Callia. 'But that is no harm; when we go back we can light it again from our own. It does not seem so dark here as it was at first.'

'I can see better, too!' exclaimed Calladon. 'Our lamp seems to be getting brighter. By and by, perhaps, it will be as bright as the great lamp was.'

'Meanwhile,' said Callia, 'let us begin our explorations.'

Holding the lamp before them, they advanced together curiously through the gloom; but, as Calladon had said, their lamp seemed continually to grow brighter, or else their eyes became more accustomed to the darkness, so that presently they were able to see

their way with little difficulty. The walls of
the room they were in were sombre and rich;
there were carved panels and cornices of
metal or stone, encrusted here and there with
what appeared to be precious stones, gleaming with a dusky red lustre. There was gold,
too, here and there ; but not bright and re-
splendent, like the gold of Abra, but dull and
tarnished, so that it might almost have been
mistaken for rusty brass. As they went
along, the black smoke from their candle rose
in the air, and collected in clouds beneath the
heavy groined roof, until it hung above them
like a murky canopy. From this canopy a
stifling odour descended, and was diffused
about the room ; but, strange to say, the
children seemed to breathe it with pleasure,
and to grow stronger and livelier under its
influence. At length they came to a great
heap of some dark substance, piled up in an
obscure corner.

'What is this ?' said Calladon, stirring it
with his foot.

Callia stooped down and took up a piece
of it in her hand. 'It shines,' she said. 'It
must be something valuable. Hold the lamp
nearer.'

'It is certainly some kind of jewel,' said Calladon, after they had examined it. 'Perhaps it is a ruby, or a black diamond. Such things are very precious.'

'We had better take what we can get, then,' said Callia; 'we shall not find anything like this in Abra—of that I am sure. How foolish you were, Calladon, never to have thought of coming in here before. It is ten times better than the other place!'

'I will fill my pockets now, at all events,' replied Calladon, 'and make up for lost time. What a heap of them! and how heavy they are! I'm afraid we shan't be able to carry them all.'

'I can hold a great many in my apron,' said Callia; 'and we can take them to some safe place, and then come back for more. I wonder whom they belong to?'

'They belong to us, since we have found them,' returned Calladon; 'and if anyone says they are his, we can say it is not true. Who has more right here than we?'

'I don't see why we should go back at all,' observed Callia. 'I feel much more comfortable and happy in this pleasant light and smoke than I did in that glaring white Abra, with its cold air and its tiresome music. Suppose we make our home here?'

'I was going to propose the same thing,' answered Calladon. 'And I have been thinking, Callia, that perhaps this is the real Abra that we are in now. For what can be better than what we like best?'

As Callia was about to reply, they heard a flapping sound in the air above their heads; and looking up, they saw a hideous great bird—or perhaps it was a bat—with black wings outstretched, fiery eyes, and a long hooked beak, that it kept opening and shutting with a snap. At this sight the children were much terrified, and started to run away; but the horrid bird followed them in the air, swooping downwards every now and then, and pecking at them with its beak, or trying to tear them with its ugly claws. At length, however, they managed to conceal themselves behind a buttress in the wall; and the bird flapped by, and left them.

CHAPTER V.

REGENERATION.

'IT will not do to stay here,' said Calladon, as soon as he had caught his breath. 'That creature probably owns the jewels, and we should never be safe from him. And I have lost ever so many of the stones while——' Here Calladon broke off suddenly, and uttered a cry.

'What is the matter?' asked Callia. 'Is the creature here again?'

But Calladon was staring at the mirror which still hung round Callia's neck, and he looked as if he had seen a ghost.

'Tell me, Callia,' he said; 'tell me quick! Am I the same as I was before?'

'Just the same, except that you look very much scared at something.'

Calladon gave a shudder. 'Then the glass tells what is false,' said he. 'It makes me seem like a hideous little deformed dwarf, with a hump on my back, and one shoulder higher than the other, and a hateful face all covered with sores and bruises. If I look like that, I must be more horrible than anything we are likely to see here.'

'The mirror tells lies, that is all,' replied Callia, scornfully. 'If I were you, I would not look in it again. I can tell you all you need to know about yourself. But I think we had better attend to getting away from here now. There seems to be a hole through the wall just where we are standing. It must lead into the next room.'

'Let us creep through then,' said Calladon. 'That flying creature will not be likely to follow us there ; and as well as I can see, it looks more comfortable there than here. At all events, it is further from Abra, and that is reason enough for going.'

'Mind that the lamp doesn't go out, then,' said Callia, 'and come along !'

They crawled through the opening (which was, in reality, one of the five windows of Cada) and found themselves standing in something soft and slippery, like mud. The walls were covered with damp mould an inch thick ; spotted toadstools grew in the crevices of the stones, and festoons of de-

caying weeds hung from the roof. There
was a low crackling sound in the air, like the
noise of burning wood, and hot puffs of
steamy vapour were wafted into the children's
faces, smelling like the inside of a pig-sty.
Strange to say, however, neither Calladon
nor Callia appeared to find this odour disagreeable, but quite the contrary ; and they
went onwards with evident gratification.

'The more I think about it, Callia,' said
Calladon, 'the surer I am that this must be
the real Abra. Could anything be more
delightful than this thick air, that you can see
as well as breathe ; and this floor, all soft and
sticky—not hard and dry like the other ;
and these beautiful walls, covered with that
curious green stuff; and then the toadstools
and the weeds ? What a lucky thing that
we thought of coming !'

'And how much wiser we are than we
were before!' added Callia. 'When I was in
that dreadful white place, I used to feel as if
I knew almost nothing, and as if the great
lamp were the only light in the world. But
now that we have a light of our own, it is
easy to see that we know almost everything,
and by the time we have explored this place,
there will be nothing we do not know.'

'This mud must be very valuable,' said Calladon, after a while; 'for I never saw anything like it before. Don't you think it would be a good thing if we were to smear ourselves all over with it, and then hang some of those lovely weeds round our necks?'

Callia was delighted with this idea, and the two forthwith sat themselves down in the softest mud-heap they could find, and began to cover themselves with mud very diligently. After this had gone on for some time, however, Callia suddenly gave a shriek.

'What is the matter?' asked Calladon.

'The snake! the snake!' cried Callia. 'It is winding itself all round me!'

'And round me too!' screamed Calladon. 'Oh, what shall we do?'

In fact, the mud with which they had covered themselves had become alive, and was coiling itself tightly about them in the form of serpents. There were already scores of them, and more seemed to be coming to life every moment. They tried to run away, but the serpents twined about their limbs and tripped them up. There seemed to be no escape; and now, to make matters worse, Calladon's lamp flickered and went out.

'We shall die!' moaned the children.
'Oh, will no one help us!'

Then a sound was heard like an earth-
quake, and the walls that separated them
from Abra were rent asunder, and a terrible
white light streamed forth, and fell upon the
unhappy children.   In that light they looked
at one another, and saw that they were deformed and hideous beyond the power of
words to describe.   The next · instant the
walls closed together again, but a faint illumi-
nation still remained, in which Calladon and
Callia again seemed to themselves to resume
their natural form.   But even then, Calladon
caught a glimpse of himself in the enchanted
mirror; and there was once more the crook-
backed, grisly-faced dwarf that had frightened
him in Cada, now made more ugly yet by the
serpent-mud of Bra.

'Oh, Callia, it is the truth!' groaned he.
'Our own eyes have deceived us, and our
lamp has led us astray; but in the mirror is
the light of the great lamp, and it shows me
as I really am.'

'Yes, it is the truth!' answered Callia.
'It must be so!'

'It is well that you have found it out,

even so late as this,' said a stern voice close behind them; and looking round, the children saw a tall, threatening figure, with angry eyes, and in his hand a heavy whip.

'Who is it?' faltered the children to each other, with trembling voices.

'I am he who built Abracadabra,' replied he of the angry eyes, brandishing his whip. 'I built it clean and wholesome, and you have made it a place of mud and serpents, and all unclean things. This dirt in which you have wallowed is the evil that has come out of your own minds and hearts, and these snakes were called into life by the light of the lamp which you stole from the lamp of Abra. Therefore your doom is, to repair the mischief you have done. You shall cleanse these rooms that you have defiled, until they are as pure as they appeared when you looked on them through the alabaster wall. From this hour, too, you shall see each other no more until your work is done. As you were given to each other for happiness, so, since you have disobeyed the law by which alone your happiness could be everlasting, you shall be separated to do your penance. And I will stand over you with the whip; and every time you pause to breathe or rest, you shall be driven onwards with a blow.'

Scarcely had the tall man uttered these awful words, than Calladon saw Callia suddenly vanish from his side ; and at the same moment he felt the heavy stroke of the whip across his shoulders, and heard the stern voice bidding him work. So to work he went with all his might ; and with his bare hands—for no tools were given him—he strove to scrape away the mud from the floor, and to clear the mould from the walls, and to pull down the decaying weeds that dangled from the roof. . But, for a long time, he seemed to make no progress ; the mud rose before him in mountains ; the mould collected on the walls as fast as he swept it down, and the weeds hung from the roof in thicker masses. Nevertheless, if he stopped to take breath or rest, down came the heavy whip with relentless blows ; his skin was cut and bleeding, his face was bruised, and the bones of his back were broken. With tears and groans he struggled on ; and ever and anon in the darkness near him his ear caught the sound of sobbing and piteous cries, and the voice that uttered them reminded him of the voice of Callia.

Thus he strove for many weary hours; and at last it seemed to him that he could strive no more, yet half his work was still undone. But the thought that, unless it were finished, he would see Callia no more, gave him new strength, and he fell to again, and worked like a whirlwind; and the mountains of mud gave way before him, and the mould fell from the walls in showers, and the dangling weeds were swept down in mighty heaps. And although the blows of the whip still fell, they no longer weakened him as before, but made his strength greater. Indeed, it seemed to him as if he were inspired with a strength not his own, and as if, when the work were done, it would be the achievement not of himself, but of a mightier than he. In the midst of these thoughts the gloom suddenly brightened, and he saw that his work was done.

'Well, Calladon, what do you think of yourself?' said the tall man, in a somewhat less stern tone than before. 'Are you as handsome as you once were?'

So Calladon looked at himself; and he
saw that he was begrimed with dirt, and that
his back had been broken by the whip, and
one shoulder made higher than the other;
and his face was bruised and covered with
sores.   There was nothing beautiful about
him.

'I have become what the mirror has
already showed me that I was,' he said
humbly.   'But I would rather seem as ugly
as I am, than seem beautiful when I am
ugly.'

'Calladon,' said the tall man again, 'your
work is done, and you deserve some reward.
You may choose what it shall be; but I will
tell you beforehand that, if you choose to be
made beautiful again as you were before, it
shall be done.'

'I would rather be made happy,' replied
Calladon, 'and it would make me happy if I
could see Callia once more.'

'So be it!' said the tall man, kindly.
'Come with me!'

He took Calladon by the hand, and instantly the light grew brighter; the dark
walls grew white; there was a sound of

music in the air, and a delicate perfume of flowers came to Calladon's nostrils. He looked up and saw that he was in Abra ; and the great lamp burned in the centre as before.

'Oh, not here !' he exclaimed, shrinking back and hiding his face. 'I am not fit to be seen in the light of Abra !'

'Take courage,' said his guide. 'Callia is here. See, she is asleep. Go to her, Calladon, and look in the mirror on her bosom.'

So Calladon drew near, and looked into the magic mirror. But instead of a hideous and misshapen little dwarf, it showed him the image of a noble and beautiful boy, with rosy cheeks and bright eyes. At the same moment Callia awoke ; and seeing Calladon, she sprang up with a cry of joy and kissed him. She was as lovely as the day.

'The mirror tells you the truth now as always, Calladon,' said the Master's loving voice—for it was he. And he laid his hand upon him, and instantly the deformed.shell in which Calladon was clothed fell from him, and he was more beautiful than ever. From

that time forth there was no unhappiness
for either Callia or Calladon, because they
had learnt that the light of Abra was the
only true light, and that their strength was
not their own.

THEEDA.

' CHAPTER I.

THE BOOK AND THE VASE.

OSCAR lived beside the sea, and had no companions except the waves, the seagulls, the sunsets and sunrises, the moonlight and the shore. He was happy, and yet there was something that he wanted. He could not tell what that something was, but he did not the less feel the need of it on that account.

He knew that he had a father, but he had never seen him. He knew that his father cared for him, and gave him what he needed to eat and drink and wear. His mother had told him that his father was wise and powerful and good; and that once, before Oscar was old enough to remember anything, he had lived with her in the cottage beside the sea. But soon after Oscar was born, his father had left them and gone across the sea to another country. When a few more years had passed, he had sent for Oscar's mother to follow him, and she had gone. Oscar could just remember the ship which had taken her away. He had sat in the cottage doorway, and watched the ship grow smaller and smaller as it receded over the waves. At first its sails had looked dark, because they were against the light; but a moment before it touched the horizon, where earth and heaven meet, the great white light from beyond had touched the sails, and made them gleam like angels' wings. Then ship and sails had settled into a lustrous invisibility; a long wave had broken with a hollow sound upon the shore, and a feeling of tender sadness had come into the little boy's heart.

Although he was alone, however, he was not lonely; there was a great deal to amuse him. The cottage, which was made out of the hull of an old fishing boat, was as pleasant a place to live in as a boy could wish. It was divided into two rooms, in one of which Oscar slept, and in the other he ate his dinner. The furniture was very simple — a bed, a chair or two, a table, and a bookshelf; but these were all that Oscar required; and besides, he spent most of his time outdoors. There were two other things in the dining-room, however, for which he cared very much. One was a large book, which lay on the bookshelf. It was a gift which his father had left for him when he went away. It was a large heavy book, with a dark binding and a golden clasp. This clasp could be opened only by pronouncing over it certain words which Oscar's father had bade the boy's mother teach him when he should be old enough. These words were a secret, and if the secret were betrayed, certain penalties would follow. It was Oscar's habit, on getting up every morning, to take the book from the bookshelf, and having spoken the magic words, to open it and read. Now, the pages of the book appeared like ordinary printed pages, and if anyone besides Oscar had looked into them, they would have read only a number of stories which were not very interesting, and which did not seem to be of any especial importance to anybody. But with Oscar it was very different; for, as the morning sunshine fell upon the page, he saw, not the printed words, but wonderful pictures, which lived and moved, and had many strange and beautiful meanings. The pictures were something like the world in which the boy lived, but much brighter and more glorious, and the people who moved in them were far nobler and handsomer than any that Oscar could have imagined; and chief among them was a grand figure which the boy recognised as his father. While going over the pages of this mysterious book, therefore, Oscar, in his lonely cottage, was able to see with his own eyes all the mighty deeds that his father had done, and even many of those that he was at that moment doing; for the book was a living book, and though it told of marvels in comparison with which all other fairy stories would seem dull and commonplace, yet these marvels were all true. By studying that book a man could become wiser than the wisest of philosophers, and see more than the greatest of travellers, and yet remain as simple as a little child. It would take a long time to tell you even a few of the wonders which this book held between its dark covers. One of them was, that if Oscar was in any trouble, he had but to open his book, and the pictures would show him how the trouble was to be overcome. Every pain that he could suffer, and every difficulty that he could meet, had been met and suffered by his father long before ; so that by seeing what his father had done, he learned what was the best thing to do himself. For Oscar was like his father, though he was but a little boy.

The other thing that the dining-room contained was a large crystal vase, which stood in the window. It had seven sides, and was so large round that Oscar could not make his arms meet about it. It was filled with the purest water, and at the bottom were sand and pebbles, and delicate sea-weeds, red and green, and pieces of rock covered with curious mosses and tinted lichens. It was like a little sea, only that there were no living animals in it. But under the shadow of one of the rocks lay a large pearl shell, which Oscar fancied must hold some living thing, although, often as he had watched it, it had never yet moved or opened. But the boy had faith and patience, and every new day he went to the vase, in the hope that now at last something might have come from the pearl shell. It lay quiet, how-ever, and kept its secret to itself. It must certainly be a pleasant secret, Oscar thought, for the shell was exquisitely curved, and its pearly sides shone with a delicate lustre.

R

And the more he pondered over the matter, the surer he became that the vase must have been given for the sake of the shell, and that by-and-by the shell would show why it was there. Sometimes he felt tempted to take it out of the water, and try whether he could see inside of it. But he could never quite bring himself to do this, because, though the vase and the shell were his own, he felt that they had been given to him to look at, and not to meddle with. In his book, too, he saw that the night always comes before the morning, and the winter before the spring; and though he did not understand why that should be so—why the morning should not begin just after the sun had set, and the spring buds and flowers come out as soon as the red and yellow leaves of autumn had fallen—yet he saw that one wave followed another to break against the shore, and that every flower was a bud before it was a blossom, and that no happiness was so happy as that which had been waited for ; so he believed that the secret of the shell would disclose itself when the right time should come, and that to try to find it out beforehand would perhaps be to lose it altogether. Moreover, was not the shell beautiful enough as it was ?

CHAPTER II.

OSCAR INSIDE OUT.

WHEN these early morning hours were over, Oscar used to go out of the cottage and wander about beside the sea. The waves murmured to him, and the sun was warm; the seagulls wheeled above his head and screamed with their wild voices ; great white clouds built themselves into cities and palaces before his eyes ; lights and shadows wavered everywhere, and made the grey rocks and the distant mountains seem alive; winds whispered in the long grass, and sang crooning melodies in the branches of the trees ; little insects and animals ran hither and thither, and seemed busy even when they were doing nothing. Sometimes the rain fell, making a secret sound in the leaves, and causing the surface of the clear pools to leap aloft in tiny pyramids; then the green plants stood up and stretched out their stems, taking their wetting gladly, and growing taller after it, though it had made them bob their heads. With the evening, splendid colours came along the sky, though the hand that painted them was not seen : they, too, spoke a kind of language ; the glories of the day that was past, and the thoughts and hopes that Oscar had had, seemed to glow in the heavens as they glowed in the boy's memory. They faded at last, and night darkened the world, so that Oscar might not forget the moon and stars. These never slept, and therefore Oscar knew that he might sleep. The rays that came from them found their way silently into his heart, and filled it with the fresh and quiet fancies that afterwards grew into dreams. For his dreams did not come from the world he lived in, but from some other.

But what was this that the waves and the birds, and the light and shadow, and the trees and the rain, and all the rest of it, were trying to say to him ? Was it really anything ? and if it were, why could he not understand it ? Sometimes he thought he almost understood it. If the things would speak a very little plainer, or if he could see

and hear the least bit more clearly, there would
be no more mystery. He thought they would
say, ' Oscar, we are like you. We are here
because you are here. If you were not Oscar,
we should not be what we are. And if we
were not here you could not speak, nor think,
nor be glad or sorry.' But they never did
quite say this. Therefore Oscar was not
quite content, and he felt that he needed
something, he knew not what, more than
the earth and the sea and the sky had given
him. They were so friendly to him that they
made him long for a nearer friendship still.
He could not come closer to them ; and if
they could not come closer to him, must not
something be wrong ? He found them always
fresh, and full of new things that never came
to an end ; they were alive, but the life they
had was not quite the same as his own life.
The world was so big that he could not put
his arms round it and hug it ; it was calm
and orderly, and although he could never get
to the end of the new things that were in it,
yet he knew that every year it was the same
world that it had been before. It was not so
with him ; for, in spite of his being always
Oscar, he knew every day that he never had

been and never would be exactly the same
Oscar that he was at that moment. So the
world was not only too big for him, but, in
another way, it was too small for him also.
The world could live only a year, after all,
since one of its years was the same as
another; but Oscar felt that he could live
innumerable years, because no one of his
years was the same as any other. Oh, if
he could only find something to love that
would grow in the same way that he grew,
and answer him when he spoke, and be in all
ways both as large and as small as he! Up
and down the shore Oscar wandered, and
through the green shade of the rustling
forest, and with his eyes he sought amidst
the clouds and the stars, but the thing that
he wanted he did not find.

When the rain came down too hard,
Oscar would stay within the cottage, and
study his book, or watch his pearl-shell, or
sometimes go into the bedroom and look
at the things his mother had left behind her.
They were very ordinary things, and there
were very few of them; but they were dearer
to Oscar than anything else. Here was the
jacket his mother used to wear, and against

which Oscar's face had often rested, while she nursed him in her arms, or lulled him to sleep. It was full of wrinkles and stains, and was torn in one or two places; but it was his own mother's own jacket, and made him think so vividly of her kind face and loving eyes and warm soft arms, that he would heave a deep sigh, and sit still with his eyes very wide open. Then there was the comb that his mother used to wear in her hair. It was made of white ivory prettily carved. Oscar remembered how his mother used sometimes to take out this comb while he was sitting on her lap, and let her hair tumble down about her shoulders; and she used to let him feel its smoothness with his small hands, and taught him how to braid it by weaving three strands of it in and out.

The feelings that Oscar had while sitting in the bedroom with these and other things that had belonged to his mother were very different from any that came to him while he was outdoors. They were less cheerful than his outdoor feelings, but he liked them better. For in thinking of his mother he forgot himself; he had been able to put his arms round his mother's neck and to kiss her cheek. She had loved him and called him by his name; he had known that no other boy could be to her what he was; she had comforted him when he was hurt or grieved; she had been made to be his mother, as he had been made to be her son. It was not so with the world outdoors—with the earth and the sea and the sky. These had been made for Oscar perhaps; but if Oscar had been some other boy they would still have remained. They belonged to him only because he was a boy, and not because he was the boy Oscar. Therefore he could not forget himself in loving and giving himself to them, as he had done in loving and giving himself to his mother. All this brought him to think that unless, out of the earth and sea and sky, something could come to him that should both bring them nearer and yet be different from them, the promise which they seemed to hold out to him would not be fulfilled. It was not a bigger or a more beautiful world that he wanted, but a world within the world, which should contain all that made the outer world beautiful and lovable, and something more besides. Such a world within the world his mother had been to him; but it was not his mother that the boy looked for, because he knew that she was gone never to return. What was it then ? Oscar did not yet know ; but now something began to stir within him that seemed to mean that the answer would not be long delayed.

CHAPTER III.

THE PEARL-SHELL'S GIFT.

ONE morning, as he was sitting with his book open upon his knees, the page at which he looked seemed suddenly to be overspread with a grey cloud. At first he could not see through the cloud, but after a while lights and shadows began to stir duskily within it, and presently he saw, as through a mist, some one walking along a lonely pathway in a forest. The mist gradually cleared away, but the face of the person was turned from him, so that it could not be known who he was. The person came to an opening amidst the trees, overspread with soft green grass and flowers of many hues. In the centre of this grass-plot was a fountain, bubbling up like living crystal from a basin of sparkling sand. Around the margin were the golden smile of buttercups and the blue glance of forget-me-nots. The wanderer drew near and bent over the fountain. Then, out of the pure water, an arm

was stretched upwards, holding in its hand a
radiant pearl. The wanderer took the pearl,
and then the mysterious hand and arm were
drawn under the water again and disappeared.
The wanderer looked at the pearl and seemed
to rejoice in it, as well he might ; for it was
the most precious of all pearls. But while he
was rejoicing, a man came up to him who,
though he had eyes and a tongue, was both
dumb and blind ; but he talked very rapidly
with his fingers, as most dumb persons can
do ; and he used his nose instead of eyes, for
he judged whether or not a thing were beautiful or valuable by smelling of it. The
wanderer spoke to this odd person, and bade
him look at the pearl and rejoice with him.
But the other shook his head contemptuously,
and said with his fingers that his eyes were
not made to see, and that seeing was all folly
and deception ; and that a good nose was
worth all the eyesight in the world. So, instead of looking at the pearl he smelt of it,
and after doing so again shook his head contemptuously, and pulled out of his pocket a
raw onion. ' Smell of that,' he said with his
fingers ; 'that is worth all the pearls in the
world !' and then he began to try to persuade

the owner of the pearl, by many clever and cunning arguments, to throw the pearl away, and take an onion in its stead. Oscar bent forward in great eagerness to see whether the owner of the pearl could possibly be so foolish as to let himself believe that the most precious pearl in the world could be exchanged for an onion ; but just then the mist arose once more, and rapidly deepened to an impenetrable cloud, and the figures of both the man with the pearl and of the man with the onion were blotted out. Oscar closed the book. All the rest of the day he could think of nothing but this 'strange picture ; and he wondered deeply whether the blind man with the onion had succeeded in making the other man as blind as himself. If only the cloud had held back a few minutes longer !

Before Oscar went to bed he looked into the crystal vase, to see whether there were any change in the shell. For the first time it seemed to him that it had really moved a little. But the light was so dim that he could not be sure. Out of the window the sea had a marvellous twinkle of moonlight over it, and the night air was cool and sweet. Suddenly, a hideous bat, with broad noiseless wings of filmy black, hovered into the room, poised itself for a moment over the crystal vase, and then flitted away again.

. The next day was one which Oscar, so long as he lived, never forgot.

He had had a strange dream during the night, and this had taken from his memory the change which he had fancied he noticed in the shell before going to bed. But now, when he went as usual to look at it, he saw that a change had taken place indeed. .

The shell was rolled over on its back ; the lid, which heretofore had closed its mouth, was open ; and the shell was empty. Oscar could see far down into the very depths of the curving interior ; it was as smooth as satin, and looked fit to house the queen of the fairies. But there was nothing in it. When, however, Oscar raised his eyes, he beheld a sight which made him draw in his breath with a long sigh of amazement and tremulous delight. The two largest pieces of rock in the vase leaned together in such a way as to make an arch, upon the sides of which delicate leaves of pink and green seaweed grew, and other broader leaves clustered together in a sort of grove further back.

Within this grove Oscar now perceived a
movement, as if something were advancing
through them. In a moment they parted,
and a fairy-like little figure floated between,
touching the sand with the tips only of her
tiny feet. Forward she came until she stood
just beneath the highest part of the arch.
She was scarcely six inches tall, but she was
perfectly formed in every part; and her face,
though it was less than an inch long, was
completely and exquisitely beautiful; and,
moreover, it looked even more good than
lovely. Her hair, which was finer than the
finest cobweb, floated around her like a sort
of brown mist; it was very thick and immensely long—nearly five inches! Her skin
was more pure and delicate than the inside of
a white geranium bud; but the palms of her
little hands had a faint rose tint, and so had
the tips of her infinitesimal fingers and toes.
Her eyes were like fairy forget-me-nots; and,
ah! who can describe that tiniest marvel of all
perfection, her mouth, with its tender curved
lips, and teeth no bigger than grains of white
sand. This little lady carried in one hand a
broad frond of green weed, which arched over
her head and protected her from the rays of

the sun that fell through the crystal sides of
the vase. Round her neck was hung a neck-
lace of seed pearls that might have come out
of a mussel as large as a millet seed. From
the waist depended a curiously woven girdle
made of thread-like sea-grasses of various
colours. There she stood, gazing straight at
Oscar with her wondering blue eyes, and her
lips half parted. And Oscar gazed at her,
almost afraid to breathe, lest she should
vanish out of his sight. For he could not
yet believe that she was real. He had never
even dreamed of anything like her before.
But he was awake, and she still stood beneath
the archway of rock, and he saw many sweet
expressions pass over her face. Yes, she was
a real, living little maiden, and she had come
into the world to make Oscar happy ; to sup-
ply the want he had felt ; to be something
that he could love and live for.

Oscar felt so tenderly towards her, and so
fearful lest he should do something to alarm
or shock her, that at first he did not venture
to do anything at all. He was so terribly big,
he thought, that she must find him frightful.
He longed to show her in some way that
there was nothing in his heart but love and

reverence for her. In the midst of his perplexity, however, the little maiden smiled a
smile that was all the more delightful because
the eyes and mouth she smiled with were so
small; and with a light movement she half
walked, half floated towards him, until she
stood close to the crystal side of the vase.
The tips of her fingers rested against it, and
she looked up at Oscar with a glance so win-
ning and so confiding that he no longer felt
any doubt about her or about himself. He
stooped down and put his lips to his side of
the crystal vase, and they kissed each other
through it.

In this way the pledge of friendship between them was given. As soon as it had
been done, the little maiden made a leap as
of joy, and then began to dance about inside
the vase, sometimes touching the sandy bottom, but most of the time gliding to and fro
in mid-water, turning herself this way and that
in graceful caprioles, diving through the archway and coming up out of the grove of sea-
weeds on the other side; waving her arms
about her head with dreamy motions; sometimes resting quietly upon nothing, as if she
were asleep; then swimming like a fish with

her arms folded and her feet crossed one over the other ; and now playing at peep-bo with Oscar behind the rocks. Oscar had never been so delighted ; his eyes sparkled and his cheeks were red. At last his little playmate dived into the pearl-shell and disappeared, and the boy began to fear that he should see her no more. But in a very short time she came out again, holding something in her hand. She smiled and nodded to him, and' rose up through the water until she nearly reached the surface. Oscar thought she must be coming out, and his heart beat with ex-pectation. But she was not coming out. Instead of that, she stretched up her tiny hand above the surface, and Oscar now saw that it held a pearl. He cautiously put out his own hand, and took the pearl from her fingers. Then she nodded again, and descended.

'Is this for me ? ' asked Oscar, very softly.

Hereupon she made him the most charm-ing little bow imaginable, at the same time bringing both her hands to her lips, and blowing him a kiss.

'Thank you, you lovely little creature !' said Oscar. ' But can you understand all I say to you ? '

S

Again the little maiden smiled, and nodded her head up and down.

'And can you speak also?' the boy demanded.

She put up one hand, and waved it slowly backwards and forwards before her face.

'Ah, she cannot speak!' thought Oscar; and he felt a momentary touch of sadness.

But at that an expression came into her face that seemed to say, as plainly as could be, 'If I cannot talk as you do, still I can talk.' And not only did her face seem to say this, but she said it, as it were, with all there was of her; and although in one sense there was very little of her, yet in another sense there was so very much, that not the largest giant ever heard of could have said so much without speaking as she could. Oscar could not account for it. Talking without speaking was something new to him. 'But, after all,' he thought, 'nobody could talk under water; and no doubt thinking under water is the same as talking out of it.' Besides, though this wonderful little water-maiden was but six inches tall, her thoughts were evidently quite as big as those of an ordinary grown-up person, so that they must be so much the

more easily visible. And, finally, why should
Oscar trouble himself about how anything
happened, as long as it did happen, and was
agreeable? Probably it was because he
already loved this exquisite fairy so much,
that he was able to understand what was
passing in her mind.

He named her Theeda—he did not know
why, except that that sounded as if it must be
her name, and she seemed to be perfectly satisfied with it. And so these two fell in love with
each other at first sight, though she lived in
water and he in air, and there could therefore be no meeting between them, except the
meeting of their hearts and eyes. They
must even kiss each other through the crystal.
Nevertheless they were as happy as the day
was long, and indeed much happier, for time
is a thing with which happiness has very little
to do. Oscar's only regret was that Theeda
could not be with him when he took his walks
upon the shore. He enjoyed his walks, however, more than he had ever before done,
because now the earth and the sea and the
sky not only said to him, 'We are like you,
Oscar,' but also, 'Theeda loves you!'

CHAPTER IV.

THE CRAB.

OSCAR could never see enough of his little water-maiden ; and he talked to her perhaps all the more because she answered him only by sympathetic thoughts. He told her all that he knew of his life before she came to him—about his dreams by night and his reveries by day ; about all the beauties of the world that she could not see from the crystal imprisonment of her vase ; about his mother, too, and how the sails of the ship in which she went away had been lit up by the light beyond just before reaching the horizon verge. He spoke likewise of his father, how good and great he was, and how, although he lived and ruled in a distant country, he never forgot to send his little son all things that were necessary for his comfort and happiness.

'And I believe, Theeda,' added Oscar,

'that he put you in the pearl-shell for me.
Perhaps you have seen him?'

Theeda threw back her floating mist of
hair, and smiled.

'Ah, of course, everybody who is good
and lovely must have come from him,' Oscar
murmured, as if answering something she had
said. And then he went on to talk about
the book, and of the strange picture he had
seen in it the day before she appeared.

'I think, now,' he said, 'that the wanderer
in the forest must have been myself; and the
precious pearl that was given to him out of
the fountain was you. But who was the blind
and dumb man with the onion?'

At that Theeda's head dropped, and she
sank slowly down on the sand, and she hid
her face in her hands.

'What is the matter, Theeda?' cried Oscar; 'dearest Theeda, what has happened?'

She partly lifted herself up, though still
crouching in the sand, and held out her arms
towards Oscar as if entreating him to do
something. And now, for the first time, he
could not read her thought. She seemed
to beseech him; but he, who would have
given her everything, knew not for what she

besought him. At last she trailed herself to the side of the vase and put up her lips to be kissed.

'I love you, Theeda!' said he. 'See! with my whole heart!'

But all that day Theeda's sadness did not wholly pass away; and each morning afterwards, when Oscar first came into the room, she would meet him with a kind of timorousness, and would not be happy until he had kissed her through the crystal, and had told her again that he loved her.

She was by no means an idle little maiden, however. The vase was her home and her garden, and she was busy many hours a day in keeping it in order and making it more and more beautiful. It was wonderful how much she found to do. In some places, where the red and green weeds grew too thick, she pruned them with a little knife that Oscar had given her, made out of a piece of a mussel shell, and cut away the pieces that were decayed. She sifted the brown sand between her fingers, and cleansed it from all impurities; and she brought the prettiest of the pebbles and laid them in tasteful patterns. She plaited a kind of hammock out of the

sea grass, and hung it at the entrance of the
archway; and in the afternoons, when the
sun was hot, she lay in it and took her siesta.
And now Oscar, from time to time, put in
little sea-animals to keep her company and
amuse her; he found many such in the rock
pools along the shore. There were prawns,
almost transparent, striped like zebras with
fine pink stripes, and having long feelers like
hairs, which they waved about, and, as it
were, asked delicate questions with them of
everything that came near. They moved as
lightly as thistledown and as swiftly as sunshine. Then there were fishes, slender little
things an inch or two long, with round astonished eyes, and open mouths that looked as
if they were saying, 'Hoo! hoo!' They
were of all colours, and some of them had
fierce-looking spines on their backs, which
they could move backwards and forwards
very much as a horse moves its ears. These
fish were at first very timid, and kept under
the shadow of the rocks, or lurked amidst the
seaweed. But Theeda soon made friends with
them, so that they regularly came to her to
be fed, and sometimes she used to play at tag
with them, darting round and round inside

the vase, and in and out amongst the rocks,
while the weeds waved to and fro like banners
in a gale of wind. Oscar also brought sea-
snails, with brightly tinted shells, which crawled
slowly about, measuring their way with their
one soft foot, and stretching out little transparent horns in front, like children feeling their
way in the dark. Besides these there was a
hermit crab, which lived in a pearl shell very
much like Theeda's, but only about a sixth
part as big. This crab was the only ill-
natured creature in the vase. He sat sullenly
in the door of his house, in a little hollow
under a large stone; his little dull eyes stuck
far out of his head, and his ugly claws hung
down in front like a pair of red fists. He
never had a pleasant word for anybody ; but,
if any came near him, he either pettishly
hitched himself back into his shell, or else
made a vicious snap at the visitor with his
claws. He even snapped at Theeda two or
three times, and then Oscar wanted to take
him out and throw him back into the sea. But
Theeda was very forgiving, and would not let
this cross little crab be punished. She always
treated him kindly, brought his dinner to him
every day, and did all she could to make him

goodnatured and comfortable. But nothing seemed to make him any better; and one day, when Theeda had made him let go of a prawn which he had caught by the tail with one of his claws, he flew into such a terrible passion that Oscar felt very glad, for the sake of the other creatures in the vase, that he was no bigger. He made up his mind to have him out before long.

Except for the crab, the vase was the most charming place to live in that could be imagined, and Oscar often wished that he were able to breathe under water as easily as Theeda did, and that he were as small as she was. Theeda, no doubt, wished so too; but it was not to be. Then Oscar used to hope that, some day, Theeda would grow up to be as tall, or nearly as tall, as himself, and then come out of the water, and live with him in the cottage. But that did not seem very likely to happen either. And perhaps, after all, they were as near together as many people who live in the same house, and are separated by neither water nor crystal. Only, when Theeda brought out her oyster-shell dinner-table, and set it under the bower of green ulva leaves, and placed upon it her little

cockle-shell dishes of fresh sea vegetables
(which was all she ate), Oscar's very heart
ached to be sitting at the opposite side of the
table and dining with her. Water then seemed
to him a much more agreeable element to pass
one's time in than air. But, although wishing
can do a great deal, it could not quite make a
merman of Oscar. Theeda ate her dinners
by herself except for the tit-bits that she
gave to the prawns and snails, and the scraps
that the fishes stole when they thought she
was not looking.

'Some day, Theeda, perhaps . . . . !'
Oscar used to say, without ever finishing the
sentence.

Theeda understood very well what he
meant, and used to look as if she meant it
also. And Oscar's father, who was as powerful as he was kind, would no doubt be able to
make them happy in the way they wanted, if
he saw that it was best for them. But the
hermit crab had a very ugly and malicious
look, as if he had a mind to prevent anybody
from being happy if he could.

CHAPTER V.

A STRANGER.

ONE morning, while Oscar was looking into the vase, and admiring the bright silver beads that were forming all over the leaves of sea-weed, and on the lichen-covered surface of the rocks; and while Theeda was busy feeding the fishes, who seemed to get hungrier the more they ate; and just when Oscar was about to remark that the hermit-crab was not in his usual hole, nor anywhere else that he could see—at that moment a dark shadow suddenly fell across the vase, shutting it off from the sunlight, scaring away the fishes, and making Theeda look up with a start, and then quickly take refuge in her shell, as from something she feared.

Oscar also looked up, and saw somebody standing before the window.

It was a boy; but a very odd boy, Oscar thought. He was not any bigger than Oscar,

but he seemed to be a good deal older. He
had a broad flat face, with a sharp little nose
in the middle of it, a wide thin mouth, and
pale eyes which stuck out very far, and over
which he wore spectacles. He had pale
reddish hair growing upright on his head.
His legs were so thin that it seemed a wonder
he could stand upon them, and indeed they
were bowed out sideways, as if the boy's
weight were too much for them. His arms
also were thin, but his hands were immensely
large and red, with stiff, thick fingers, and
huge thumbs. He was not quite facing the
window, but stood sideways towards it, and
looked at Oscar askance. The skin of this
boy's face was coarse and rough, and seemed
as thick as orange-peel.

'What is your name?' asked the strange
boy, after a while.

Oscar told him what it was.

'What an absurdly old-fashioned name!'
said the boy, contemptuously. 'I have a
better name than that—my name is Kanker!'

'Do you want anything?' said Oscar.

'Yes,' said Kanker. 'I want to ask questions. I am in search of truth. I never
believe lies; so you needn't tell me any.'

' I never tell lies,' said Oscar, gravely.

' That is a lie to begin with. Everybody tells lies—except me! Everything lies—the things that can't talk, as well as the things that can. The world is a lie.'

' The world is not a lie,' said Oscar, indignantly. ' And if you think it is, why do you search for truth ? '

' I have at all events found the only truth there is to be found—and that is, that everything is a lie,' replied Kanker. ' I have proved it a thousand times already, and every new question I ask proves it again.'

' What makes your hands so big ? ' Oscar could not help asking.

' They are no bigger than they ought to be,' Kanker answered, holding them up and looking at them admiringly. ' I use them to touch things with. I never believe in anything that I haven't touched. Nothing exists unless I can touch it. Come out of that room, so that I may touch you, and see whether you exist.'

' I will come out,' said Oscar ; for he thought it would be better to go to Kanker than to have Kanker come in to him. ' But you need not touch me ; I can touch myself if I want to.'

Nevertheless, no sooner had he come out than Kanker took hold of him by the arm, and gripped it so hard with his big red hand that Oscar said, 'Let go, you hurt me!'

'Your touching yourself would prove nothing to me, you know,' said Kanker. 'Well, you seem to exist. Where are your father and mother?'

'They are not here,' answered Oscar. 'They are gone—long ago.'

'I don't believe it. Where did they go to?'

'Over there,' said Oscar, pointing across the sea.

'Nonsense! Do you mean they are drowned?'

'No. They are gone to a country over there.'

'How do you know there is a country over there? Did you ever touch it?'

Oscar shook his head.

'I thought so. Then there is no such place. Therefore your father and mother have gone nowhere. Therefore they do not exist. And what business have you to exist if you never had a father and mother?'

'I don't know what you mean,' said Oscar,

'and I don't care whether I exist or not, so long as I do what is right, and am happy.'

At this Kanker laughed, a spluttering laugh, as if he had his mouth full of water. ' Sit down here beside me,' he said, ' I want to ask you.some more questions.'

Oscar sat down beside him. He did not at all like Kanker, whose voice was as harsh as his manners were impolite. And he was certainly ugly. When Oscar did not look full at him he had something the appearance of a gigantic crab, which was increased by his sidelong shuffle in walking, and by the two great red hands that he carried hanging before him, very much as a crab carries his claws. He held a sun-umbrella over his head, a small book in one pocket, and a roll of measuring tape in the other. Nevertheless, Kanker seemed to know so much, and to be so positive about what he knew, that Oscar could not help thinking he must be an important person ; not the sort of person to be contradicted, especially by a person who knew so little as Oscar did. ' For, after all,' Oscar thought, ' a great deal of what I supposed I knew has only been told me. I do not know

it as he knows things—by touching them. It
may be, as he says, that some things that
seem to be true are not true. I wonder
whether he believes in the sun and the stars?
He can hardly have touched them! And I
wonder why he wears spectacles?'

'Why do I wear spectacles?' repeated
Kanker; for Oscar had spoken the last sentence aloud.. 'To see with, of course! Nobody can see without spectacles; and not only
that, but nobody can see with any other spectacles than these I have on.'

'Oh, you are mistaken there,' exclaimed
Oscar; 'for I have never worn spectacles,
and I have always been able to see.'

'You never saw anything in your life,'
replied Kanker, very confidently. 'You only
think you see. That is your hallucination.
An hallucination is when you think a thing is
so, and it isn't. You are blind, and probably
deaf and dumb as well. What books do you
read?'

'I have only one book,' said Oscar; and
then he told what a wonderful book it was; how
it could only be opened by repeating certain
mystic words, and how its pages were full of
living pictures, representing things which had

been done in the world, and which were being done now.   Kanker burst out laughing. '

' I don't believe it,' he said.   ' It's an hallucination.   There is no such book, in the first place, and if there were, it couldn't be what you say it is.'

This made Oscar angry.   ' There is such a book,' said he, ' and if you don't believe it I can show it to you.'

Kanker went on laughing and wagging his great hands up and down.   ' Oh ! show it to me—show it to me !' he spluttered.   ' Let me touch it with my fingers, and then perhaps I'll believe.'

' Come into the house, then, and you shall touch it !' exclaimed Oscar.   He sprang up and went into the house, and Kanker followed him readily enough.   ' Let me put my fingers on it—that's all I ask,' he kept repeating. ' Let me touch it.'

' There !' said Oscar, 'there it is on that shelf.   Do you believe now ?'

Kanker took the book down from the shelf, and felt it all over.   ' I believe that this is something that feels like a book,' he said at last.   ' But I don't believe it is a book until I see it opened ; and then I shan't believe it

T

has the pictures you talk about unless I see them, and can put my finger on them ; and I don't believe you can open it.'

'I can open it!' cried Oscar.

'If you can do it, then why don't you?' Kanker replied.

Now Oscar knew that the mystic words which undid the clasp were a secret which he had no right to disclose. But he wanted so much to show Kanker the inside of the book, and make him acknowledge that he was wrong, that everything else seemed of little account in comparison. He took the book from Kanker's hands. As he did so, a strange feeling came over him. A voice, that seemed to speak not to his ears, but within him, bid him pause. Did he care so much for this Kanker, with his flat face and his great red hands, as to betray the secret which his mother had confided to him ? Oscar hesitated.

'Ha! I knew you were lying!' said Kanker, with his disagreeable laugh.

'You shall see that I am not!' retorted Oscar, becoming angrier than ever. Then he began to repeat the mystic words. But he found it hard to pronounce them, and some of them he could scarcely remember.

His teeth chattered as he went on, and his heart beat painfully. But Kanker was watching him askance with his pale spectacled eyes, and Oscar would not stop. At last he had spoken all the words; the clasp flew back; the book opened!

'There!' said Oscar, thrusting it into Kanker's hands. 'It is open : now look for yourself!' Then he turned away, and hid his face in his hands.

All of a sudden he heard again Kanker's hateful spluttering laugh. He looked up in astonishment. Kanker was pointing contemptuously to the page.

'No pictures here!' he was saying. 'Show me your pictures! There's nothing but printing here, and very stupid commonplace printing too!'

Oscar fixed his eyes upon the book; but they were darkened, and at first he could see nothing. At length his sight cleared; but, alas! it was as Kanker had said : there were no pictures in the book, no beauty, no life, and no mystery. It was just like any other book—ordinary pages printed with ordinary print. There had been some terrible loss, but whether the loss were in Oscar or in the book, Oscar could not tell. He stood there unable to speak, and almost to think.

' It is just as I knew it was,' said Kanker, throwing down the book. ' Another of your absurd hallucinations. You dream about things until you think they are real. You had much better do as I do—wear spectacles, make up your mind that everything is a lie, and trust to your fingers. By doing that you might, in the course of time, come to know something. Look here, I'll tell you what I'll do. I'll make an exchange with you. It isn't a fair exchange, for what I give you is worth a great deal, and what you give me is worth nothing. You give me your book, and I'll give you mine.'

' What is your book ?' Oscar asked.

' An arithmetic, to be sure !' replied Kanker, pulling it out of his pocket. ' See, here is the multiplication table. And here are addition, subtraction, multiplication, and division. And here are vulgar fractions. And here are examples. And here is the Rule of Three. That's what I call a book worth having.'

' But if you think my book is not worth having, why do you want it ?'

'To make a fire to warm myself with,' Kanker replied.

'If you are cold, will not the sun warm you?' asked Oscar.

'No one has been able to prove that there is any warmth in the sun,' said Kanker. 'It only seems to be warm. But I know that a fire is warm, because I can burn my fingers in it.'

'But if the sun feels warm, is not that as good as if it were really warm?'

'For you it may be,' answered Kanker, 'but not for me. I care only for truth, and I don't choose to be warmed by anything I don't believe in. That is the reason I carry a sun-umbrella. Well, will you let me have your book?'

'It is no more use to me,' said Oscar, gloomily. 'I do not care whether you take it or not, or what becomes of it.'

'You will find my arithmetic much more useful,' returned Kanker. 'Come outside and see me make my fire.'

But Oscar turned sullenly away.

Kanker went outside the cottage, with the book in his arms. After a moment, Oscar could not help going to the window to see what was being done.

Kanker had laid the book across two stones, and had gathered some bits of drift-wood from the shore for kindlings to put underneath. Now he struck a match, and held it to the kindlings. But at that there was a sudden and mighty sound, like thunder, and also like a great voice speaking some solemn and awful word. And the book seemed to dissolve, and in its place arose a tall pillar of light, more dazzling than the lightning, which hung for a moment near the earth, and, to Oscar's amazed eyes, took on the likeness of a glorious and majestic figure, which bent upon him a look that made his heart tremble. Then the figure moved away through the air seaward, casting a radiance across the waters, and making the sun look red and dim. It drifted slowly away over the sea, and at last became as a bright star, further and further off, until it vanished in the depths of the sky. Then a great coldness fell upon Oscar, and the daylight became dusky to him, as if it were already evening ; and he knew that the dazzling face which he had seen was the face of his father. Now he understood what the book had been ; but it was too late.

CHAPTER VI.

THE SECRET OF THE WAVES.

IT seemed to Oscar that many hours passed away while he remained crouched down on his knees in a dark corner, shivering and miserable. At last he looked up. It was evening, and a bitter wind was blowing outside; heavy clouds were driving across the sky, and rain was beating on the roof. Kanker was sitting in the middle of the room, with his chin upon his hands, staring at him.

'You had better go,' Oscar said. 'What other harm do you want to do me?'

'It is you who have done harm to me,' replied Kanker, 'by giving me a box of gunpowder to make a fire with. The explosion has cracked my spectacles. However, I bear no malice. What do you keep that jar of sea-water for?'

'Ah! that is where Theeda lives,' exclaimed

Oscar, rising, with some cheerfulness in his
face. ' I had forgotten her.'

' Theeda ? what is Theeda ? ' demanded
Kanker.

' She is my playmate and companion,'
Oscar said. ' She is dearer to me than anything else in the world, and nothing in the
world is so lovely as she.'

' And do you mean to say she lives in the
water ?   Pray, how big is she ? '

' She is not so tall as your hand is long.'

' No such creature ever existed,' said
Kanker, positively. ' In the first place, no
one ever was made of that size, and in the
second place, it is impossible for anyone to live
under water.   It is another of your hallucinations.   There is no use in your denying it.   I
shall believe in her when I see her, and not
before.'

' I will not let you see her,' replied Oscar.

' Just what I expected !   When did you
see her last yourself ? '

' Just before your shadow fell across the
vase.'

' What language does she talk ? '

' She does not talk at all, but I know all
she thinks.'

'This is really too absurd! Have you ever touched her?'

'No. It is enough for me to look at her.'

'I will tell you what it is,' said Kanker, lifting up one of his ugly fingers and holding it at the side of his little sharp nose. 'You are crazy—quite crazy! You have lived here by yourself until you don't know what is real from what isn't. Now, I will make this bargain with you. If you will let me put my finger on this Theeda of yours, and I thereby prove to my own satisfaction that she exists, I will let you use me for your servant the rest of my life. Do you agree?'

Oscar waited a little while before answering. He hated Kanker, and he thought that if Kanker became his servant, he should be able to make him as miserable as Kanker had made him. He did not stop to think whether Theeda would like to be touched or not; it seemed to him an easy way of being revenged on his enemy, and that was all. 'Yes, I agree!' he said.

'Very well!' returned Kanker. 'And, of course, if I prove that Theeda does not exist, you are to become my servant for the rest of your life?'

'There is no danger in my promising that,' said Oscar. 'Let it be so if you wish.'

'Very well!' said Kanker again; and then they both went to the vase.

'Where is she?' asked Kanker. 'I don't see her.'

'Oh, she has gone into her shell; it is late—she must be asleep by this time,' answered Oscar. 'You must wait until to-morrow.'

'That won't do!' said Kanker. 'The agreement was for this evening. If you back out, you become my servant.'

'It shall be this evening, then,' replied Oscar; 'but you will regret it more than I!' And stooping over the vase, he called, 'Theeda! Theeda! wake up! come out!'

They waited a moment. There was no movement in the great pearl shell, and Theeda did not appear.

'Come! there's enough of this nonsense!' Kanker exclaimed. 'You may as well make up your mind at once to being my servant.'

'Not yet!' said Oscar, scornfully, and he called in a louder voice, 'Come out, Theeda! Come out—I want you!'

The shell stirred slightly, but still Theeda did not appear. Kanker laughed.

Then Oscar grew angry, and in a harsh tone he cried, ' Theeda, come out! or I shall not love you or believe in you any more!'

The sun had set long ago, and the sky was almost dark ; but now, through a break in the clouds, the moon shone down, white and clear, into the crystal vase. It gleamed upon the pearly shell ; and in its cold lustre Oscar saw the tiny water-maiden, whom he had loved better than anything else in the world, and who was the most precious thing that the world contained, come slowly out of her shell, and stand downcast and drooping before him. Then he felt that, in his anger, and in his desire to be revenged on his enemy, he had done a wicked thing, which could not be forgiven. He had shown what was most sacred and dear to his own soul to one who could neither believe in her nor reverence her. His heart was filled with bitter sorrow and repentance ; but again it was too late.

For, as Theeda stood there in the moonlight, drooping amidst her shadowy mist of hair, Kanker put out his hideous red hand, that was less like a hand than like a crab's claw, and plunging it into the water, he tried to grasp Theeda round the waist. But his fingers met together, and behold! no Theeda was there. She had faded into nothingness where she stood; or else the shadow of a cloud which at that moment passed across the room, and made the vase and the room dark again, had caused her to become invisible. Before she disappeared, however, she bent one sad reproachful look upon Oscar, and he knew that he had seen his mother's spirit in her eyes. He understood all then; but it was too late indeed!

'I told you how it would be!' said the harsh voice of Kanker, with his spluttering laugh, 'and now you are my servant!'

'Yes, for I have lost my Theeda!' answered Oscar, with a heavy sigh.

But even as he spoke, he chanced to turn his eyes towards the sea. Beyond the moon he saw a pure white cloud drifting down the sky. To Oscar's fancy it took on the likeness of a female form—the form of someone whom he knew and loved. She seemed to beckon him to a far-off country, whither Kanker could not come, and where he would be free.

' Yes, I will follow her!' Oscar thought; and, in some way, he slipped from where he was, and left the cottage and Kanker behind him, and went down towards the ocean.

Kanker did not at first know that Oscar had escaped, for he had left something behind which resembled him, but was not really he. The next morning, when the sun peeped as usual into the crystal vase, neither Oscar nor Kanker were to be seen. But, in the pearl shell, where formerly Theeda had lived, sat a great ugly crab, twiddling its huge red claws, and peering this way and that with its malicious little eyes, which stuck far out of its head. Oscar was not in the cottage, nor on the shore, nor has he, from that day to this, ever reappeared there. But, if you should ever happen to visit the place, you will hear the waves murmur mysteriously to one another, as they gambol along the beach; and since they come from that far-off line where the world meets the sky, they may possibly know more about Oscar and Theeda than people like Kanker would be apt to believe.

THE END.

Spottiswoode & Co., Printers, New-street Square, London.

www.ingramcontent.com/pod-product-compliance
Lightning Source LLC
Chambersburg PA
CBHW020859020726
47497CB00005B/1484